THE EVENT
LITTLE DRAGON

What readers say

*"This book is a combination of the Karate Kid and Rocky.
Master Wong is a combination of Daniel Son and Rocky Balboa.
This is the ultimate in what martial arts is all about."*
GRANDMASTER - John Hackleman (Pit Master)
Founder of The Pit Hawaiian Kempo

*"A very good story, well written and interesting. It's easy
to get absorbed in the story and forget it is about
Master Wong's early life.
I'm looking forward to more in the future"*
GRANDMASTER - Samuel Kwok
Traditional Ip Man Wing Chun

"Good book, great story, a tough life journey."
Will Henshaw
World of Martial Arts Television

*"An inspirational story of self-discipline and self-motivation.
Master Wong goes from
'Coming from NOTHING' to 'Becoming SOMETHING'!"*
Sal Mascoli
IDO Consulting

*"It's powerful yet liberating, leaving you
Tormented yet cleansed - wanting to read more."*
Jazz Gill
Founder / CEO - SPARBAR®

"Awesome page-turning narrative. Raw, open and gripping."
Paul "Chuck" Norris
Bush Adventures UK C.I.C

THE EVENT

BOOK 1
LITTLE DRAGON

OUR GOALS ARE ...

The purity of your intent, the focus of your will, the level of your awareness, the quality of your character.

MASTER WONG

THE EVENT

BOOK 1
LITTLE DRAGON

www.masterwong.tv

Foreword

I have known Master Wong for many years, first as a teacher and then as a very close family friend. Indeed, I regard his family as our family and it is, therefore, not only a privilege to be asked to write this foreword but one I do most gladly.

Let me first turn to the man, Master Wong, before discussing the young boy in this story and its central theme of bullying. During the course of my 40 years' involvement in martial arts, I have known many senior, world-class martial artists from various disciplines and of all of them, in my opinion, Master Wong is the real deal. He knows what he is talking about and he can walk the walk. He has been there.

Now to this wonderful book. Master Wong vividly brings to life the trials and tribulations of young Hung from the very early age of 6, suffering unbelievable beatings from gangs of local boys. Beatings too from his mother, but my guess is that he probably deserved at least some of those that he had from his mother – although perhaps not quite so viciously as he received.

I asked myself what I was doing at the ages of 6 and 7 - my first and second years at school – and I think the worst thing I ever did was fart loudly in class and not own up to it, resulting in the rest of the class being kept in detention. Even then, no classmate took it out on me. When I think back, I did not experience bullying of any kind, in and out of school, until about the age of 11 when I was on the receiving end of a judo stomach throw from the school bully.

I see clearly the reasons why Hung suffered such bullying - the fear that was prevalent amongst everyone at that time in Hung's part of Vietnam. The power that the bullies felt that they could exercise over Hung and others. Hung's ethnicity. All these reasons, in the same forms and different ones, still relate to our society today.

Bullying comes in many varieties, both physical and mental. It happens at home, on the street, in school, at play and at work. Although I agree the best fall-back is to be fully prepared in terms of self-defence, there is another aspect of self-defence which is avoidance of trouble. That is something I learned very early on, which is why I have only had one real fight in my life: it is not always necessary to fight fire with fire, but who knows what will be the outcome when your back is against the wall, or your loved one is in a life-threatening situation.

I have no time for bullies and nor does Master Wong. If this book helps just one young person to understand and identify the dangers around him or her and how best to deal with those dangers, then Master Wong has, by writing this excellent and gripping book, done what he set out to do.

Trevor Gilbert OBE
6th dan karate - Shihan

The Event
Little Dragon

by Master Wong

Copyright © 2019
All rights reserved.

No part of this book may be used or reproduced in any manner whatsoever without written permission except in the case of brief quotations embodied in critical articles or reviews.

Acknowledgements

The Master Wong team would like to thank all the people who have made this book possible. This is but one step of many that our team is taking - working as one in different countries to bring this book together as part of our aim to combat bullying wherever it is found, worldwide. We hope that everyone involved with the project feels proud and fulfilled by a job well done. We want to give special thanks to the following individuals for sacrificing their time and putting special effort into this book to ensure its success.

The Master Wong Team:

<u>Author</u>
Master Wong

<u>Co-Writers</u>
Philip Chute
Douglas Turner

<u>Additional Thanks to</u>
Antoine Swift
Lindsey Hess

Dedications

This book is dedicated to all Martial Artists in the world who strive to protect people in need and also to those who help others who are weaker and more vulnerable than themselves. Most importantly, this book is for the victims who suffer bullying, whether at school, work or home.

This is a problem that we feel needs tackling and confronting every day because the number of people it affects, from all walks of life, is increasing. Bullying through online forums and social media outlets is also becoming a significant worry that also needs to be dealt with by all of us, working together.

May this book give you the courage, inspiration and determination to rise and take action!

We hope this book will bring you the knowledge to change what you thought you could not.

OUR LOVE AND STRENGTH TO THE WORLD

DISCLAIMER

This book is set in the 1970s and early 1980s. It contains frequent details of violence and physical injury. Reader discretion is therefore advised and parents should consider whether the material in this book is suitable for younger children.

In particular, reference is made on a number of occasions to the beatings that the young Hung received from his mother.

This book is largely factual but some names have been changed. The majority of events described in this book actually happened. However, some of the descriptions and the background to certain events have been changed, purely to make the narrative flow better. The events that you will read about happened to Hung - Master Wong - during his early childhood, growing up in northern Vietnam. The repeated beatings that are described in this book really happened. It was a tough upbringing.

However, Master Wong wishes it known that he bears his mother no ill-will for the treatment he received from her during his childhood - or at any other time. The beatings that she gave him were, in the view of the adult Master Wong, largely deserved!

In addition, both the time and place have to be borne in mind: parents physically beating their children was normal in Vietnam (and much of the rest of the world) in those times. Other children in Master Wong's home village were chastised as much, if not more, than he was by his mother. Master Wong is telling his story as he felt it happening to him.

Times have changed and expectations of parental behavior are different now... but what is acceptable now is not what happened in those times. Standards of behavior change and Master Wong is determined to tell the story of growing up in the tense and difficult times then in Vietnam, without sentiment and without pulling any punches.

The book has been written for a worldwide audience. So for some readers, there may be words and expressions with which you are unfamiliar. Master Wong trusts that this will not reduce your enjoyment of the book - and he advises that if you don't understand any words or phrases, then apply your Martial Arts' disciplines and be practical and resourceful...

You should look them up!!

WARNING: All of the techniques described in this book are dangerous to use and should not be attempted by any one who is untrained or undisciplined in Martial Arts.

Explanation of Names

This book is set in Vietnam and is about the early life of Master Wong. Upon his arrival in England, he adopted the name "Michael" to help him settle into his new life in a foreign land. Michael is a popular English name. However, Master Wong was - and is - also still known to his family, both in England and in Vietnam, by his original given name of Hung.

Therefore, the name "Hung" is used in this narrative so that it fits better with the life that Master Wong was living at that time and to be consistent with the name that he was called by those around him. Similarly, Vietnamese names are given to most of the other characters described in this book, although where local people were given Westernized nicknames, these have been used.

PROLOGUE

Vietnam/China Border

The Vietnam War was a conflict that caused untold suffering in Vietnam itself - and also in neighboring Cambodia and Laos - over twenty years, finally ending in April 1975. The number of deaths is estimated at anything up to 3.2 million. The final figure will never be known. The War is remembered for many things, not least the use of Agent Orange and napalm.

However, the tragedy continued. The communist regime which had fought out of northern Vietnam had taken control of the largely capitalist southern provinces of the country. Huge numbers of people from the south were sent to camps to be "re-educated".

Land, businesses and houses were confiscated. Rape, torture, forced relocations, looting... Even murder was common. It was as if it was becoming the norm.

Living conditions were grim. Mass unemployment spread across the country. Hunger and starvation was rife. People felt that they had no future. Many, with great sadness, turned their thoughts to fleeing the country; it broke their hearts, but they saw no future for themselves in Vietnam.

Getting out of the country was virtually impossible. However, desperation can trigger an acceptance of extreme risks. Thousands of people started to leave Vietnam, by whatever means they could. The vast majority took to the seas and became what we know as "The Boat People".

Less well known is that towards the end of the War, in January 1974, a clash between Chinese and Vietnamese forces resulted in China taking control of the Paracel Islands.

Political tensions escalated. China and Vietnam share a land border of nearly 1,300 kilometers and, as if the people hadn't been through enough already, from 1979 to 1990, a border war was waged between the two countries following the breakdown of peace talks.

On February 17, 1979, the Chinese Liberation Army crossed the border, causing devastation in parts of northern Vietnam and threatening the Vietnamese capital, Hanoi. Both sides suffered heavy losses; there were thousands of casualties.

Vietnam fortified its border with China and stationed as many as 600,000 troops there. China stationed approximately 400,000 troops on its side. Fighting along the border took place from time to time throughout the 1980s. China then threatened to launch another attack to force Vietnam's exit from Cambodia.

It was terrifying for the people living in the border provinces of Vietnam. Countless numbers of men and women died. Horrifying atrocities happened: children and babies were caught up in the fighting. Many were orphaned: some became orphans while still at the breasts of their mothers.

Whereas after the Vietnam War, it was largely from southern Vietnam that many of the Boat People started to flee, now the exodus spread further across the country, up into the northern provinces. Once again, families were torn apart. Some were separated for months – for years. Others were never to see their loved ones again.

Countless thousands drowned at sea, fleeing Vietnam in flimsy, leaking, overcrowded boats. Despite the risks - the virtual certainty - of drowning, pirate attacks, starvation, thousands were prepared to risk all for the hope of a better life, free from attacks upon them and their families and loved ones. The loss of all that they held most dear.

The era of Vietnamese Boat People lasted fifteen or more years. No one knows how many tried to escape and more to the point, the number of deaths is unknown, but it has been estimated at half a million or even more.

This book is set around the time of the late 1970s and early 1980s, which was the peak of the mass exodus of Boat People.

CHAPTER ONE

By the time he reached six years old, Hung figured that his life had already gone to Hell. His hair had stopped growing; it had been long, tangled and knotted. It proved impossible to tease out the knots so they were cut out ... that was if the hair hadn't already been pulled out by the roots, either by Hung himself or others during fights. So his head was shaved: he figured being bald was better and gave his attackers less to get hold of.

On Hung's sixth birthday, Vietnam was still at war with China. There was a cultural war within his family too; his mom being Vietnamese, his dad Chinese. They lived in what Westerners would call the slums of northern Vietnam and everybody hated the Chink-eyed, half-breed kid and his family.

That morning, Hung woke to the sounds of things breaking inside the shack that was the Wong family home. He was used to these sounds. He'd hardly notice the noise, since it happened so frequently.

There was always a nagging, uneasy, feeling in the pit of his stomach - fear. Fear: the constant demon that only went away when he was falling asleep but not quite dreaming yet: that time of calm when the head seems to drift into a feeling that it is floating. Fear sucks ... in more ways than one.

Hung wasn't the only one in his family to have this demon

inside him; all but the youngest member of the Wong family felt that the fear demon had him or her in its claws.

In both size and height, Hung was a small boy, even for a six-year-old. He was always quiet and sometimes could be rather naive about life, especially when it came to what poor families such as his had to do, just to survive. During the day, the majority of his time was spent cooped up in the shack, away from the rapidly increasing racism going on around them in Hon Gai, Quảng Ninh Province, Vietnam.

Their home village was becoming a more violent and dangerous place to live: conflicts between families in the village itself and conflicts across the Province and in much of northern Vietnam were happening more and more as the Vietnamese people tried, time after time, to claim their full independence from China. As part of their efforts to do this, the Vietnamese were starting to push out anyone who was Chinese or part Chinese. Violence ran unchecked throughout the country and bullying became common everywhere, against both adults and children.

"You're half-Chinese, half-Vietnamese. There's no place for you here, you Half-Breed bastards! Piss off! Get out of here!"

Hung tiptoed up to the doorway of the main room of the shack. His mother was inside, busy cleaning up broken glass. His father was shouting and swearing at her. More stones had been thrown through the windows. Hung could hear his father yelling something about a boat and them leaving because they were not welcome in the village. Somehow or other, Hung's younger brother, Quân, had stayed asleep through the racket.

LITTLE DRAGON

Suddenly another stone flew in through the window, breaking his mother's favorite flower vase, before rolling across the floor. Despite all the troubles going on around them, Hung's mother had always tried to have one or two vases of flowers in their home, to try to brighten it up. Now she had only one vase left. His mother looked so sad: another small spark of happiness had gone.

The fear demons squeezed his stomach and twisted inside him harder and harder. Hung didn't understand what his parents were talking about, but he knew it wasn't good. He wanted to go into the room, to be closer to his mom and dad, but the fear demons wouldn't let him. It felt as if his feet were glued to the floor. It seemed that he was stuck - so he stayed put, rooted to the spot, in the doorway. He just watched …

During the days that followed, Hung started to notice little things were going missing, such as his mother's wedding ring. His father was collecting small pieces of gold wherever he could find them, both in their home and from other places – not that Hung knew anything about them. He understood enough to know that if they were to be leaving and had to pay for things, it would be easier to use gold to buy what they needed. His father seemed very keen to leave, but at the same time Hung could see that he was very upset about the idea of doing so. Hung didn't mind at all: he had always wished they could move away – from the village, the Province. He wanted to go far away. He couldn't imagine any place worse than this horrible village where they were being treated as enemies by so many of their neighbors. He hated too the horrible hill where the village stood.

LITTLE DRAGON

Looking back years later, it seemed to the adult Hung that when he had been living in his home village, it was as if his world was upside down: when he climbed slowly up the hill, home to the shack, it was like he was walking downhill... down into Hell, where there was nothing but misery.

Large numbers of drunks, bullies and violent men would take advantage of the local women: bashing them, stealing from them and, worst of all, raping them. They beat up anyone who tried to intervene.

While home life was full of misery, walking down the hill was grim too; that was like entering a cave where demons lived. Hung knew that for Chinks like him, there would be nothing but trouble – every day.

A few days later, while his mother was cleaning the shack, her eye was caught by a movement outside. She looked out of the window: she saw that one of their neighbors, who was also part-Chinese, was making his way down the hill. The neighbor was a tall and skinny man - even more skinny than the rest of the villagers. His eyes were so sunk into his head that he looked as if he was almost dead. It was clear that he hadn't eaten much, if anything, for a long time: he was so thin that he couldn't walk upright. He was walking slowly and clearly was in a lot of pain. His body shook and trembled from the effort it was taking. But somehow, he still staggered on his way.

Hung's mother hurried over to the door. She dragged it open as fast as she could, almost pulling down the front wall of their home with the force that she used. As all her attention was on the door and the neighbor outside, she didn't see Hung creep out of the shack. In one corner of the room where Hung and his brothers slept, the corrugated iron of the wall had come loose from the frame. There was a gap between the iron sheet and the wooden frame, just big enough for Hung to squeeze through. Hung had been using it for some time as a secret way in and out of the shack.

Hung's mother shouted at the neighbor: "Hey, where are you off to? You're not well enough to be going anywhere, are you? You shouldn't go down the hill: you won't have the strength to come back up again,"

"They beat up my boy. They broke his hand," he said. His voice was weak and feeble and he trembled as he spoke. "Then they forced him to come home and steal what was left of rice and take it back to them! I've got to get the rice back, otherwise we'll have nothing to eat."

"They'll KILL you!" Hung's mother screamed at the sick man. She saw that it was getting dark outside: that would make matters worse for him, she was sure.

She could hear a group of men walking up the road. She could tell they had been drinking because they were yelling and singing and the words were slurred. The neighbor turned towards the rowdy thugs: both he and Hung's mother could see that they were looking for trouble. They were bragging about beating up some young kid.

Then the old man heard what he was expecting: one of the guys boasted, with an evil grin on his face: "Yeah, you heard the crack when I stood on his hand? It was loud, wasn't it?" Another of the thugs beside him laughed: "I can't believe the kid actually brought the rice back to us. I bet his folks were pissed with him."

Hung's mother could make out at least four different voices. She looked back at her neighbor. The expression on his face went from one of exhaustion and feebleness to one of rage. She watched him straighten his back and ball up his fists. He started walking down the hill again, towards the voices.

"Stop!" Hung's mother pleaded with her neighbor. "They'll kill you!"

The man looked over his shoulder. "Yes. Yes, they probably will. But if I let them get away with bullying me or my son, then I might as well be dead."

One of the gang, a tall, thin, man known to the local folk as "Slim", saw the old man walking down the hill towards them. He saw both the determination in his eyes and the anger and fury that seemed to leap out at them from his face.

"Who the hell's this guy?" he asked the others, pointing along the road in the old man's direction.

"I don't know, but he looks pretty hacked off!" said Lanh, the biggest of the thugs. They looked at each other, as if to see if they were all thinking the same thing, then they burst out laughing. They started again to walk up the hill towards the village, ready to meet the old man.

Lanh stepped out in front of the pack a little. They were now only a few paces from the weak and furious old man. Lanh stopped in front of him: he had a big smile on his face. He opened his arms wide.

LITTLE DRAGON

"What's the matter, Little Man? Do you want something? Can Lanh help you, Daddy?" he asked, talking to the man as if to a child. He sneered at the old man. The others started to surround him, spitting on the ground in front of his feet.

Lanh was not expecting what happened next. Without missing a beat, the old man stepped in and twisted his body slightly. With what seemed like the speed of lightning, he flashed a fierce punch with his right fist that caught the big asshole bully square in the solar plexus! Lanh stumbled back a step: his breath and a small amount of vomit spewed out from his wide-open mouth.

The older man didn't pause; he shifted his feet, twisted his body in the opposite direction and fired the palm of his left hand straight up into his target's chin. Lanh's head whipped back and at the same time, consciousness left him. His body went limp as he fell backwards. He was out cold before he hit the ground - hard. A grin of pleasure crossed the old man's face while, for the briefest moment, he stood over the unconscious man lying at his feet, waiting to see if he was going to get up. Then suddenly, without warning, it seemed that the old man's strength left him as quickly as it had come to him. The adrenaline rush that had given him both strength and courage wore off and his body sagged over. He looked his age again.

Two of the three remaining thugs stood frozen in shock from what they just witnessed. Slim, however, took advantage of the old man's short-lived joy at having beaten the chief thug and snuck up behind him. He pulled out a stick like a police baton from the back of his pants and, with huge force, swung it down onto the old man's head. Thwack!

Blood flew everywhere, splattering over the attacker's

face and chest. The old man's skull cracked: it sounded like an egg shattering. The other two younger men joined in the attack, kicking viciously at the unconscious man's head and body. They didn't let up.

By the time they had finished torturing the old man and felt that he had been paid back, most of his teeth were missing and both his hands were broken. The old man no longer moved. Was he breathing? They didn't know or care – and none of them bothered to check to see if he was. The three thugs picked up Lanh, who had finally begun to regain consciousness, before heading back down the hill.

Hung could hear his mother calling for him. He'd watched what had happened to the old man. He had seen him die in front of him. The shock hadn't really set in yet. He couldn't understand why the man went to fight the thugs in the first place. Four fit and strong young men against one tired, ill, starving old man.

Hung heard his mother calling his name yet again. She sounded cross. He hurried back to the house, pushing his way through the bushes where he had been hiding, back to the gap in the wall of the shack. He snuck back inside and pretended to be playing with Quân. He was just in time: his mother walked into the room to check on him.

There were more vicious attacks in the village the next morning and in the days and weeks that followed. Every day, Hung woke up from a horrible nightmare only to realize that he was living in one. Much of the violence was carried out by men – and some women – who, at first glance, appeared to be soldiers. They were a ruthless organization of Vietnamese Communists who wore uniforms like soldiers and who made sure that the villagers never felt safe or secure. Life was lived on the edge, all day and every day, whenever the Vietnamese soldiers were around.

The attacks got closer and closer to the Wong family home. Hung watched a truck-load of the Vietnamese rebels working their way through the house of a nearby villager, stealing or smashing up all his possessions. He could see the mother of that family, standing outside the house, getting drenched in the rain. She watched what was happening with tears in her eyes. There was nothing that she could do to stop it: she was powerless – and helpless - but she still tried her best to protect her children and to shelter them both from the rain and from what they were seeing was happening to their home and to their family.

The woman's Chinese husband and his brother were being clubbed again and again to a bloody pulp. Their shack was ripped down by the soldiers, who then started doing it all over again to the Chinese families in the neighboring shacks.

Luckily, Hung's father and older brother had crept out of the village and headed to the local harbor earlier that morning, just before the latest round of thuggery, beatings and thieving started. The two of them reached the harbor only to see hundreds of refugees desperately trying to get on the boats. These people were trying to get away. Somewhere – anywhere. Anywhere that was away from Vietnam.

After Hung's father had sold everything that he could – nearly all of their possessions – there still wasn't enough to pay for the whole family to get on one of the boats. They were only able to collect enough gold and other items of value to get two of them onto one of the leaking boats. Hung, Quân and his mother had no choice; they would have to stay on and wait longer. Staying in the village which had become even more of a Hell to them now. How long would they have to wait?

At the dockside, Hung's father and brother watched people rushing towards the dock workers who were collecting the huge bribes for boarding one of the boats – none of which were really in good enough condition to be taken out to sea with just a small crew on board, never mind when over-full with hundreds of refugees on each one. The folk who tried to force their way onto the boats were beaten up by the dock workers or by the crews and they were thrown into the water, unconscious. No sympathy was shown: even young women with babies in their arms were tossed into the water as well, if they had no money for a seat on a boat, no matter how much they begged for help.

Up and down the coast and even in the harbors, bodies floated in the water, drifting back and forward on the waves as if they were taking part in a ghost-like dance of death. The calls and shouts of the people - the yells and screams of terror - echoed around the harbor, sounding from a distance like the whistles of an express train. There was much fighting both on the boats and the docks. Both Hung's father and brother were on the receiving end of dozens of punches and beatings with sticks and canes as they fought their way across the deck to a corner, which they claimed as their own. At least they then had two sides, protected by railings, from which attacks were less likely.

To make matters worse, even though they had bribed the crew to let the two of them on board, rather than the five they wanted, they were almost out of money.

Their boat and one other headed out together into the China Sea, hoping to find a container ship or other large ocean-going vessel which would rescue them, either by towing them along to a friendly port or, better still, letting them on board to take them onward to another country - a place of safety. They would then send for Hung, his mother and little brother as soon as they could.

By the third day, Hung's father had seen at least five or six people on their boat simply give up and die. There was no ceremony to mark their deaths; they were simply thrown over the side - where within minutes they were eaten by sharks.

They had been joined by other over-crowded boats, trying to form themselves into a sort of convoy or flotilla, in order to provide a better chance of protection against pirates. They saw a man on one of the other boats desperately drinking seawater. The man looked as if he was going mad; he was panicking.

"He'll die of thirst," said one of the other refugees who was sitting alongside Hung's brother. It was hard to understand the man: his voice was more like the croak of a frog due to dehydration. Everyone was exhausted and they felt sure that they would die of thirst soon.

Then, without warning, one of the other boats hit a big wave that hadn't been spotted by the crewman on duty until it was too late. The boat rose up suddenly and seemed to twist on the top of the wave. The unexpected movement tipped overboard the man who was still leaning over the side,

LITTLE DRAGON

scooping up water with his hands to try to relieve his thirst.

Hung's father and brother watched as that boat continued on its way, leaving the man to drown. He was weak so it didn't take long for him to stop struggling and to sink beneath the waves.

Their boat and most of the others in their group were carrying at least 150 people each, all desperately trying to escape to freedom ... That was until Thai pirates attacked and destroyed one of the other boats, while those on the remaining ships watched what was happening with horror. There were no survivors from the boat that was attacked.

It was no picnic either for Hung, his mother and his younger brother who were still in the village. If they thought that what they were going through at that time was tough, they didn't know that life was about to get much – much – harder and grim for them.

CHAPTER TWO

Countless numbers of bodies washed up with each tide at various places along the shores of Halong Bay, even in and around the harbor at Hon Gai. People gathered along the shoreline, fighting to rifle through the torn and tattered clothing of the victims and to loot the bodies for whatever they could sell in the nearby shops.

On some days Hung's mother would come home, exhausted. She was worn out from looking to see if the bodies of her husband and her eldest son had washed up on the local beaches. Whenever she could, she took the opportunity to collect a few items of flotsam and jetsam to sell for a bit more rice: anything that had even the smallest value was taken off the beaches and traded for food and other essentials for the family.

Hung was confined to his room as much as his mother's authority could keep him there. It would have been a lot easier for her if he didn't sneak out of the house anyway. Even from the age of three or four, Quân was left alone in the house for most of each day if Hung wasn't at home. There was no alternative and no one else to care for the young children.

LITTLE DRAGON

Months went by, but there was no contact from Hung's father or older brother. It was to be years before Hung and his mother heard from them. Hung kept struggling along, barely surviving in the increasingly harsh conditions in which the family was living. Conditions that he and his mother had no choice but to accept. Either that or they would have to move on again. The Vietnamese kids kept up their bullying of Hung. That had become a daily way of life.

No one can live like this forever. If they were going to survive, they would have to leave. On the streets, in the stores and shops and even in the schools, Chinese people were kept apart from the Vietnamese: they were bullied, beaten up and tortured - all in the name of getting the Chinese the hell out of Vietnam! Needless to say: Half-Breeds were no exception to the rule.

When he was eight, Hung started to carry with him a small pocket knife, given to him by his father as a birthday present before he left. It was small, slightly rusted and the blade had been chipped in several places. He thought he would never have the courage to use it, but he knew he needed it. Having it made him feel better all the same - plus it came with a sheath which was really quite smart: it looked better than the knife itself.

One day after school, Hung was on his way back up the hill, heading home from the market. He was hurrying as fast as he could. His mother had sent him to get a couple of gardening tools to replace those that were stolen from their home the night before. He didn't expect for it to take so long, but the market was crowded. He looked around the whole of the market carefully for the tools his mother requested, only to find that he had spent most of his time searching for something the market traders didn't have. The evening was turning into dusk already. Hung was out of breath from trying to make it home before dark, but that wasn't happening.

Hung approached the alley that led up to the hill to his village, just before the sun's comforting rays disappeared and left him stranded in the gathering gloom. It felt as if the demons in his head were taking human form, ready to gang up on him in the shadows of the alley. Hung gazed into the darkness, knowing he had to go in. He could feel the demon in his stomach squeezing, its grip getting tighter around his insides, but it was more common sense than anything else that made him realize that if he didn't get home, those men up the road would get him anyway.

He could feel fear flooding his blood with adrenaline. His knees and hands started to shake, out of control. Hung took a deep breath and closed his eyes while he exhaled. "Nope, that didn't work," he said to himself. He was still scared.

He stuck his hand in his pocket and unclipped the knife from its sheath. He gripped the sheath tight to stop his hands from shaking. By the time that Hung forced himself to step forward, sweat was dripping down off his forehead and his knees were wobbling uncontrollably.

As he entered the alley, the darkness seemed to wrap itself around him like a ghost - an evil specter. The strong smell of ammonia, piss, old vomit and cigarettes filled his nostrils like a foul-smelling poison. Vomit rose up in his throat: he covered his mouth in an attempt to stop it from finishing its journey.

LITTLE DRAGON

"Yeah, that's the way I feel about you Chinks being here," a voice whispered from a few paces up the alley.

Startled, Hung swallowed back his vomit almost instantly. Now he had to try his best not to piss himself. Seconds later, the darkness released a figure that loomed forward towards him.

"Don't think this is the place you're looking for, little boy. Why don't you go home, you Half-Breed Chink?!" Hung slowly began backing up. While mentally working his way through his retreat plan - such as it was - he bumped into another, older, kid who was in the process of sneaking up behind him.

The boy grabbed Hung's head and pulled him down towards the ground, intending to hold him down. In a panic, Hung pulled out the knife from his pocket and thrust it back over, behind his head. He had forgotten to remove the knife from the sheath as he struck his opponent in the eye, but in a panic, the other boy reached for the knife. Instead, he only grabbed hold of the sheath, accidentally removing it just as Hung was pulling back for another thrust.

Hung stabbed his blade back behind him a few more times before he noticed blood trickling over his hand. He felt the boy release his grip. Hung spun around to face him. The boy dropped to his knees, looking at his hand. It was covered in blood. One of his eyes was starting to close.

Hung had managed to get some deep stabs into the boy's hand. He watched the blood pouring from the stab wounds. Another figure walked up from behind and grabbed Hung's shoulder, violently spinning him around to face him. This boy was even skinnier and had longer arms and legs than the others. He smiled: it was an evil menacing grin. Then, without warning, he sent the back of his hand across the side of Hung's face. Hung felt the heat from the boy's knuckles striking his cheekbone. Swelling of his cheek started almost immediately.

Hung would have fallen to the ground if it wasn't for the other older boy who still had a hold of his clothes. The boy pulled back, balling up his fist to give Hung a really hard punch when suddenly Hung thrust the knife into the boy's side, leaving him screaming in agonized pain.

Despite the blade being dull and chipped, it sliced through the layers of the boy's skin quite easily. The older boy let go of Hung's clothes and clasped his side with both hands. Falling to one knee, he tried to keep the blood from continuously gushing out. Hung didn't stop to look; he turned around quickly and pushed through the other boys lining the sides of the alley.

As Hung ran, he could hear his heart pounding louder and louder in his head. His tired muscles began to strain under the burden of running so long. He finally made it home, gasping for air. He rushed in, hiding the swollen side of his face from his mother so that she wouldn't scold him. He told her that the market didn't have what she wanted and ran to his room.

His mother tried to scold him anyway, but Hung went straight to his sleeping pad and pretended to be asleep. He kept his sobs quiet so his mother wouldn't hear. Finally, his body crashed from exhaustion and he eventually fell into an uneasy sleep.

Late the next morning, the pain from the side of his face

woke him up. He stood up from his pad but his muscles took their revenge by sending waves of pain throughout his body. He was paying the price for all the exertions of the events of the previous night. The pain lessened as he continued to move around, until he was left with a noticeable limp. He didn't hear or see his mother, so he assumed that she had already left to earn what little money she could. Quân was playing with some sticks and a feather that he had found somewhere: he was, even at his very young age, used to entertaining himself.

Just after midday, Hung began cooking rice for himself and Quân when suddenly he heard crashes coming from a couple of shacks along the track. He dropped the little metal cup of water he had been holding and rushed to look outside to where the commotion came from. What he saw made his heart sink.

Two really big thugs and the guy he had stabbed in the hand were standing there. One of the three - known, with some justification, by the name of "Psycho" - had taken hold of an older man and was continuously slapping him and yelling at him for information. Hung already knew what questions he was being asked. That's when he saw the signs of another bad day coming his way. The old man pointed towards Hung's house. Hung quickly ducked down from the window, grabbed Quân and started sneaking towards the back of the shack.

The first rock came through the window, smashing the last remaining pottery dishes they had. Then, all of a sudden... BANG!! A much larger rock smashed into the side of the shack, then another, and another, until it sounded like a hailstorm had struck. The sound started to become too much for Hung to handle: he slipped out of the shack, using his escape route, dragging Quân with him. He hid them both behind a pile of timber a short distance away. Fortunately for both of them, even though he must have been terrified, Quân realized how much danger they were in and kept silent.

Kneeling, Hung watched the thugs kicking in the door. It swung open with a loud metallic clang like a broken bell. The force of the kick tore the door off one of its hinges, leaving it swinging open and leaning halfway down towards the floor. Psycho walked up to the shack, closely followed by the other two. They ducked down, entering through the low door frame, pushing aside the broken door. The third of them was a bit behind the others and in trying to catch up, rushed in but forgot to duck, bashing his head on the rusty metal door frame and putting a big gash across his forehead.

"Shit!" he bellowed in anger. "Where the hell is the fuckin' kid? He's walking dead!" he yelled, pulling a rag from his pocket and holding it to his forehead. The gang of thugs glanced around the corners of the shack where the sleeping pads were but found no one there.

"It's empty," one of the thugs stated, right before Psycho smacked him across the back of the head.

"Obviously," Psycho yelled at him. "Thanks, genius!" he jeered with all the sarcasm he could muster. His friend blew off the remark; he was used to the abuse from Psycho and really didn't care anymore.

"Take anything of value and break everything else. If I can't shank the little prick, I'll starve him out... and his mother."

Hung could hear them smashing all their meager possessions inside the shack. He watched while they started throwing broken pieces of furniture out of the window. The smashing and breaking went on for about half an hour, with Hung watching them in silence from outside the window. He knew that his mother would be home soon and he knew he was screwed, no matter what.

There would be no way he could clean up and fix everything in time. Hung couldn't believe they were still inside; he didn't think they owned that much stuff to break! As soon as these thoughts entered his mind, he heard the thugs exiting the shack and heading off down the hill.

Hung waited a while; he wanted to make sure they weren't waiting for him. He left Quân hidden and went back into the shack, alone, by his secret escape route. He had to push a few things to one side in order to get back in through the tiny gap, because of the debris scattered all over the floor. Hung rushed to pick up everything and tried to clean up, to make things as neat as possible.

Within minutes his mother walked in, shocked. She saw Hung on the floor, picking up fragments of broken furniture and pottery. Hung looked up. His mother saw the bruises on his face from the night before. That's when her look of surprise changed to anger.

"I knew it! You just won't listen! How many times do we have to keep on moving on, to different provinces, always having our stuff taken, because of your fighting?!"

She swooped down and lifted Hung up so fast he hardly saw her move. She snatched him by the arm and dragged him outside, where she tied him to a tree so he couldn't get away. She brought out a thin branch that she kept in the corner of their shack, which she used as a broom. She whipped it down across his shoulder. He let out a short cry but held the rest of his pain inside. Hung had been through this before and was desperate not to show signs of weakness. He cried to himself silently during the rest of his beating.

After his punishment, Hung was sent to his sleeping pad - or what was left of it.

"AND STAY THERE!", his mother screamed.

Hung lay on his bed, curled up in the fetal position, trying to start the painful recovery from the injuries his mother and the thugs had inflicted upon him. His mental injuries were another matter. He didn't dare think that it couldn't get any worse, but he knew his demons would find a way to prove him wrong. His mother continued cleaning, picking up from where he had left off. He was half aware of Quân crawling back in via the secret hole and lying down on his sleeping pad, across the room from Hung. His mother had been so angry with Hung and so intent upon starting to clear up the mess that she hadn't noticed that Quân had not been in the house.

All Hung could do was lie on his bed and worry about the boys coming back to finish the job.

CHAPTER THREE

Hung kept on getting into trouble and so his mother sent him to work in the rice fields that belonged to her brother - Hung's uncle. They all lived in the same village - at least for a time. They would be forced to move on again - as a result of what happened next.

Working for his uncle was both good and bad for Hung: it was good to get away from the beatings of his mother and when he was out in the fields, it was easier to see when trouble was coming - the local thugs. His main job was looking after his uncle's two water buffaloes - making sure that they were fed and had water and also to wash them down daily. He also had to take the buffaloes from their holding pen and out to the rice fields where they would be put to work, pulling the plough.

Ploughing with the buffaloes was a filthy job. Mud went everywhere - on man and beast. The buffaloes liked getting muddy: it helped keep them cool, as well as making a barrier to the millions of biting insects which plagued them. Flicking a tail or ears was only a short-term fix to relieve the torture of the flies that buzzed around the two buffaloes from dawn to dusk. The flies would get into their eyes, their ears, up their noses, in their mouths and also into any cuts or wounds on their bodies - and then they would bite and, whenever they could, lay their eggs under the buffaloes' skin. Maggots wriggled about under their skin - then flies would emerge, from where they had hatched. Every morning both buffaloes would try to roll in the mud to coat themselves in it.

This caused problems for Hung: first, the mud stank. Farmers always spread shit on the fields to make the rice grow faster and to produce bigger crops. The shit was from their animals: pigs, chickens and buffaloes and even from the dogs that everyone kept. And human shit too. Nothing went to waste.

The shit took time to rot down. It lay on the surface of the fields and the hot weather made it stink even more. It was also in the standing water that the buffaloes had to wade through so when they rolled in the mud, they were covered in what was, to Hung's nose, shit.

The buffaloes stank anyway, with their own "buffalo stink". It was disgusting: it got up Hung's nose and into his skin, it seemed. Hung struggled not to throw up when he had to work with them. Washing never seemed to shift the stench. While the mud helped keep the flies from biting the buffaloes and getting into their noses and ears, the smell from it attracted insects to the buffaloes anyway, so they were always surrounded by a buzzing cloud. Of course, because the flies couldn't get through the mud to bite the buffaloes and feed on their blood, Hung was the next best target.

The buffaloes' bodies were the home to countless ticks and fleas. If Hung brushed up against either of the buffaloes, then not only would he be coated in the stinking mud, but he could also be sure that all sorts of bugs would have leapt onto him and would try to dig into his skin. Painful and very itchy.

And another thing - while most tame buffaloes are fairly

laid back, the odd one... isn't. It was Hung's bad luck that one of the buffaloes was mean and always angry. This one was a fucking nightmare: pushing Hung around with his head - and big horns - or kicking out at Hung or anyone else who came into range, especially when having his harness put on. Hung reckoned this bad-tempered sod with its evil eye had it in for him. Hung called him "The Bastard". Even that felt too kind sometimes.

Late in the afternoon on a hot and sticky day, Hung was bringing the buffaloes home from the fields. Hung had had to work in the fields all day; walking up and down, leading one or other of the buffaloes to keep them working hard. He was knackered.

He decided to climb onto one of the buffaloes and hitch a ride, leading the other one who would follow behind, at the end of a rope which was tied to its nose ring. Hung was tired, but he wasn't stupid enough to get onto The Bastard. He got on the back of the other buffalo, a sleepy and lazy beast who Hung called "Blossom". An inappropriate name, as Blossom usually stank worse than The Bastard.

Sitting on Blossom wasn't easy: she was fat and Hung's legs were short. He felt as if he was trying to do the splits but it was better than walking.

They set off for home. It was a slow journey but Hung wasn't bothered: it was good to have even a short rest. Blossom didn't need to be steered; she was as keen as Hung to get home to food and water. Even The Bastard wasn't being difficult for once; he followed them, plodding along at the same pace. He seemed to be thinking his own thoughts.

"I bet he's hatching some shitty trick to pull on me," Hung

thought to himself, giving The Bastard more credit than he deserved for intelligence.

They hadn't gone far when Hung saw, coming towards them, another water buffalo, also with someone on its back. The rider was a boy, about 16 or 17 years old. Like Hung, he was wearing only shorts and a *nón lá*, the traditional Vietnamese farmer's hat. He too was covered in insect bites and red, angry-looking lumps and spots where the ticks and fleas from his buffalo had bitten him.

The track was narrow: Hung realized that Blossom and the other buffalo would be passing very close to each other. Getting off the track wasn't an option: there were deep ditches on both sides. The other buffalo was huge: it would be a tight squeeze for them to pass on the track.

The other boy had seen Hung. All seemed normal, but as they got closer, the face of the other boy changed, from boredom to increasing anger: he had seen Hung.

"What's his problem?" Hung wondered. *"I'm going to find out."*

As Blossom and the other buffalo got closer, the boy started shouting at Hung. It was the usual abuse: "Fuck off back where you came from, Chink. No one wants you here. Piss off, you little prick. Get out of the way".

Blossom stopped. Right alongside the other buffalo. They were head to tail: Hung was directly beside the other boy, knee to knee. The track was so narrow that Blossom and the other buffalo were effectively wedged together - it seemed that if either moved, they risked falling into the ditch.

Suddenly the other boy reached down to his side, away from Hung, and then lashed out at Hung. He had picked up a thick bamboo stick - the sort used by the farmers to prod their buffalo. He brought the stick down hard on the back of Hung's head.

Hung's head snapped forward. He saw stars and felt that he was going to black out. Somehow, he didn't but that meant that the pain from the strike immediately speared through his head like red-hot daggers. Before he could do anything, the boy struck him again and again. Eight or nine times in total, all of them across the back of Hung's head and his shoulders. The pain got worse and worse. Blossom wasn't moving and because Hung's leg was wedged between the bellies of the two buffaloes, he couldn't throw himself off the back of Blossom and into the ditch.

It was looking grim for Hung. He was barely conscious. Blood was spurting out of the back of Hung's head. However, the boy was growing tired from swinging the stick. He dropped the stick onto the ground and reached over, grabbing Hung around the neck and pulling him sideways. Once he had Hung off-balance, he changed grip and put Hung in a headlock. Even though Hung's head was covered in blood from the beating, the boy managed to get a tight hold. He was strong and Hung quickly found it hard to breathe. He was in trouble.

Then the thug changed tactics. He broke the headlock and pushed Hung's head down, between the two buffaloes. He started punching Hung on the back of his head again, this time using his fists. More and more blood was flowing from the back of Hung's head. The thug was getting covered in it. Hung's head and shoulders were jammed between the thigh of the other boy and the stinking, muddy and fly-blown belly of Blossom. His breathing became more difficult - and having his face pressed into the leg of the thug did not help. He was also at risk that Blossom and the other buffalo might move even closer together, in which case Hung's head would be crushed. He had to do something quickly.

All Hung could see was the bare leg of the other boy. He couldn't do anything with his arms: because of his twisted position, one arm was out of range for him to punch the thug and the other was trapped underneath him, in the tiny gap between the bellies of Blossom and the other buffalo. Hung's nose and mouth were being pressed into the flesh of the other boy's leg, cutting off air to his lungs.

What weapons did Hung have? None that he could think of. Through the pain, his eyes gradually focused on the other boy's leg. He could only attack the leg - but with what? His mouth.

Hung twisted his head a little, so that he was looking straight at the boy's thigh. He forced his mouth open as wide as he could and then bit down - hard - into the boy's quadricep. Hung clamped his jaws together then pulled away. Blossom had shifted her weight to one side just enough to give him room to pull his head away from the boy's leg. As he did so, his teeth cut through the flesh of the thug's leg, chopping out a large chunk - a mouthful - of the thigh.

Hung saw the gaping hole in the boy's leg and the blood that was pumping out of it. It ran down the sides of the buffaloes. Some started to cover Hung's arm. Hung was shocked and horrified in equal measure. He became aware that something soft, warm and sticky - a squashy shape - was still in his mouth. He felt some of the blood from the lump of thigh dribble down his chin. It suddenly registered what he had done. He felt disgusted and a bit ill. In an instant, he spat it out onto the track.

Time seemed to stand still - it seemed like an eternity to Hung. There was silence. The thug had stopped punching the back of Hung's head. He looked down at his leg: he couldn't believe what he saw. Blood was pouring out of the wound: it pumped out with each heartbeat. A couple of smaller veins and a few capillaries had been torn - there was a steady flow of blood.

After the initial shock and surprise had passed, the pain hit the boy. He screamed - and kept on screaming. He let go of Hung who recovered from the shock quicker. He pulled himself upright on Blossom's back.

The screaming also woke up both Blossom and the thug's buffalo: both of them were startled and bolted straight ahead: somehow, they managed to pass each other. Blossom was so full of fear that she galloped at full speed, so The Bastard had no choice other than to follow her, otherwise he would have had the ring pulled out of his nose. Hung too was shocked by the screams. He didn't think to let go of The Bastard's rope that he was holding: he had enough to deal with, just trying to stay on Blossom. If he had fallen off, it was likely that he would have ended up under the hooves of The Bastard who was right behind them.

Blossom was not going to be stopped, by Hung or by The Bastard. She galloped as fast as she could, back to the pen next to Hung's uncle's house. Hung couldn't do anything to help the thug, even if he had wanted to - which he didn't. For the next few minutes, Blossom was in charge.

Hung didn't find out what had happened to the other boy

for a few days. He was expecting there to be trouble - and there was. Typical: the boy was the son of the head man of the next village. Somehow or other, despite the pain and the blood pouring from his leg, he managed to stay on the back of his panicking buffalo until he got home. By the time he got there, the shock of the injury to his leg and the loss of blood had made him feel dizzy and light-headed, so when his buffalo finally pulled up, he fell off onto the ground. His mother saw her son arrive, so was able to wrap the leg and apply a tourniquet tightly above the wound to stem the blood loss. The nearest doctor was sent for.

Being head man of his village, the thug's father knew a lot of powerful people. People who were high up in the local authorities and others who were in the police. The thug gave them a description of Hung - omitting, of course, everything about how he had attacked Hung. It didn't take the police long to work out that it was Hung who was the troublemaker: the one who had made the unprovoked attack on the "innocent" older boy.

Since the boy and his family were so well connected with those who could make life difficult for Hung and his mother - and uncle too - Hung was lucky that the policeman, who came to see his mother a few days later, was tired of having to deal with what he saw to be squabbles and pointless fights between two families. He couldn't be bothered with all the hassle that he would have to handle if he got heavy with Hung. Life was too short - and he could do without all the form-filling. The policeman had enough power to avoid having to take Hung to jail, even though the thug's father wanted Hung locked up and the key thrown away.

However, the policeman made it clear that he had heard about Hung getting into trouble before and he didn't want him around. Like most of the people in the village, he also didn't like Half-Breeds either and he wanted Hung and his family to clear off, away from the area. Hung's uncle was worried about what his friends, neighbors and other villagers would think about Hung staying on, now that he was known to be violent, thanks to the thug's story. Because he had to keep face with his neighbors, he told his sister that Hung couldn't come to his house or work for him anymore and that she, Hung and Quân would have to leave the village and move away. Again.

Hung's mother was, as expected, furious with Hung. She was tired: it was so difficult keeping Hung, Quân and herself fed and with a roof over their heads. She had thought that moving near to her brother would help and giving Hung work to do would keep him out of mischief. No such luck.

She gave Hung the beating that he was expecting, then started to collect together their few possessions, ready for them to take to the road. Once again, she would have to try and find somewhere for them to live. Somewhere where the people hadn't heard of Hung. Somewhere where having children who were part Chinese and part Vietnamese was not a concern to the local people.

Hung never found out what happened to the thug on the water buffalo, but somewhere out there is a man with a bite-sized chunk taken out of his leg.

Hung dreamt often of staying in one safe and secure place for a while. Even when he was in bed at night, he would always dream that there was some kind of trouble brewing that would cause the family to become nomads once again and which would force them, time after time, to move on from one province to another. That was the only life he knew: his family had been forced to move on, like drifters, frequently - ever since he could remember. Being a Half-Breed family was the problem. Like his mother, Hung always hoped that one of the provinces in Vietnam would treat them like regular people and that they would be accepted, at least in some small way.

As Hung got older, he thought things would become easier. Since he was becoming bigger and stronger, he thought that the neighborhood bullies would not dare to bother him anymore, but that was never going to happen: it could not be further from the truth. The bigger Hung got, the bigger the bullies became.

CHAPTER FOUR

By the age of nine, Hung was well aware of the different ways and means by which people were separated and set apart from each other. People were segregated more and more, forced to move into small communities where everyone was the same nationality. He also knew where this was most likely to happen - especially in school. Hung stepping onto school grounds was, of itself, an immediate trigger for harassment to start.

Psycho and his gang continued to give Hung grief regularly - and frequently: it was rare for Hung not to be suffering from some injury or other, thanks to the attentions of Psycho and crew. He had to defend himself alone as best he could: after that first fight over a year before, Psycho knew not to take on Hung by himself: there would always be at least two or three others to help him do his dirty work. This was all the more important from Psycho's point of view since, while Hung was still so much smaller than the members of Psycho's gang, he had the advantage of speed and natural fighting skills. Because he was almost always fighting by himself and also usually on the losing end for that reason, other kids were spurred on to have a go at Hung in whatever way they chose.

"Why don't you piss off home?" a nerdy kid with glasses told him one day. It was a statement - a command - not really a question.

LITTLE DRAGON

"*Even the nerds?*" Hung thought to himself.

"*Yeah, fuck off home*", another kid shouted, laughing at Hung.

Tranh and Duong were Vietnamese twin brothers. The only time there was any peace for Hung in school was when he was hanging out with these two. But he only did so because others thought the twins were even stranger than everyone else - including Hung. And since they were pure Vietnamese roughnecks, no one in their class dared to bother them.

Only these two Vietnamese, out of countless hundreds, seemed even to consider that Hung might be a human being. Only they, out of everyone at the school, seemed to see Hung first as a boy, not first as a Half-Breed. Hung never really thought of them as his friends until the day the three young rogues together received their first Beat Down from a group of thuggish Fifth Graders.

Hung couldn't always find the twins, but he knew that if they were around and kept together, then getting bullied was less likely to happen. This was the problem: somehow, he had to figure out how to become stronger and to fight better so he could protect himself and his friends from the tormentors who plagued them.

Sometimes Hung told Tranh and Duong about the latest beating up he had suffered from Psycho and his gang, as well as showing off his injuries. While they didn't say as much, it was apparent that the twins were impressed by how Hung stood up to the bullies and somehow had the energy, strength and courage to carry on. They would have loved to give Psycho a taste of his own medicine for all the pain he had caused... But how?

During one early afternoon after school, while the three lads kicked up dust as they wandered through the fields near the village pond, Tranh playfully threw a wild, wide and hard hell-maker left-field punch at Hung's arm with all the strength he could muster.

Hung laughed. "You know, one of the benefits of getting beaten up so much... I can take a punching from the best of them. All that you can dish out, anyway."

Without so much as a blink, Hung retaliated with a flurry of punches all over Tranh's body. Duong watched. Tranh's mind could not comprehend the number of hits his body received in less than five seconds. Squirming on the ground and in pain, Tranh looked up at Hung, shocked by the lightning speed of the attack he'd just endured. Both he and Duong learned a lot about Hung in those few seconds.

Hung's skin became tough and leathered from the continuous battering he was getting from the local thugs, day after day, and also from the need for his body to heal itself repeatedly. The nerves were so deadened and unresponsive from the never-ending shocks they had to bear that he noticed he could hit the side of the school building with his legs and his arms and the pain wasn't even half as bad as it had been. His tolerance for pain seemed to be becoming superhuman. He became extremely toned, with lean muscle developing from constant running and fighting. His muscles contained a force of strength which was, at that time, both unused by him and also unknown to him. His tightly bound muscle structure was more defined because he had almost no body fat, mainly due to lack of proper food.

Hung made it into the school grounds but didn't see his friends anywhere outside the buildings. However, he did see the usual bullies combing the outside yard, looking for anyone they could take advantage of. Hung decided to stay back for a bit and stood behind a large tree until he saw the four bullies' attention target a poor, unfortunate little Chinese boy.

The Chinese kid was known as Chinky, because at the time when he started at the school, no one had thought to come up with anything better. Within seconds, he was on the ground. Two of the bullies ransacked his pockets, searching for anything they could take.

"I'm not holding him down for nothing. There'd better be something here for me," exclaimed the third village punk who was kneeling on both of Chinky's arms. A fourth kid stood at a distance, acting as a lookout for adults or anybody else stupid enough to interfere and try to help the Chink.

Many brutal kicks and vicious punches landed on Chinky before an adult came over and pulled the Vietnamese kids off him. Mrs Le, a large and heavy dinner lady, began scolding the fighting boys, then dragged them into the school building.

Mrs Le marched the boys into the office of the head-teacher, Mrs Nguyen - a woman who always looked tired and worried. She was well used to having to try and deal with fighting at the school and its after-effects. Usually her punishments and remedies had no long-term effect and may of the more regular bullies saw it as something they could boast about: the more they were taken in front of Mrs Nguyen to be told off, the more some of the younger kids looked up to them.

After Mrs Le had given her an earful about the kids and what they had been doing, Mrs Nyugen marched the fighting boys and all the other students in their classes into the biggest classroom. She was angrier than a broken wasps' nest.

"Since everyone seems to want to fight or to stand around and watch fights, that tells me that you lot haven't enough to do. You can now do something constructive with your time. Go to your classrooms, take out your math books, go to Chapter 3 and answer all fifty questions at the end of that chapter. Then you are to complete the tests set out in Chapters 4, 5 and 6. No one leaves until everyone has finished!"

The children's faces turned sulky and glum. Everyone began filing slowly into their classrooms, their heads hanging low, frustration setting in as they thought about the work they had to do to complete their punishment by the end of the day. They sat at their desks and got their heads down.

Hung snuck out from his hiding place and ran into the building, mixing in with the rest of the kids who weren't being punished.

"Meet up with us later, Hung. We've something to tell ya", Tranh shouted, slapping Hung on his shoulder as he rushed past, catching up with the other Vietnamese boys. His two friends ran past him into the school building.

"Yeah, this is gonna blow your friggin' mind, man!" Duong shouted, punching Hung's other arm and running past him towards the classrooms. Hung gave them a confused look while watching them shoving their way through the other kids into the building.

Another younger boy ran past Hung and bumped into him as he continued walking into the building behind the twins. They were always instructed to enter the building in order, from oldest to youngest. The rule really sucked in this particular situation, because the older kids' classrooms were just inside the front door of the building. The ages of the kids' classes became younger the further you went down the hallway and of course, the older children made it torture for the younger ones to get to their classrooms. The older ones would line up along the hallway, sitting on the benches which lined the walls, while waiting for their classes to start. They would stick their legs out to make the younger children crawl under them to get by. At the start of the corridor the older boys, thirteen and fourteen years old, were always waiting. Waiting to give a good punch in the stomach or kick to the legs.

Sometimes they would kick the younger pupils so hard on the leg that they would give their victims what the kids called a dead leg. However, the older pupils usually targeted the stomach - for the pain factor. They never really hit the face, because they didn't want the teachers to see bruises. Even though the teachers usually didn't do much about the violence, leaving no visible marks made life easier for the bullies: if a teacher did take an interest, the air of innocence was easier to maintain if injuries were hidden under shirts.

After running that gauntlet, the kids went into their classrooms to start their first lesson. This was what happened to Hung every day.

Because of Hung's awareness skills and because he had learned to keep on the ball and alert at all times, on most days he made it through the gauntlet relatively easily, when compared to others. He was used to watching out for any trouble that was coming his way. Sometimes a clueless, unknowing, new kid would try to push through the line and fight back when he was attacked. That usually didn't end well; they would become the victims of 'Bully Beat Down'.

Every now and then, a teacher would do the unthinkable: something dumb like being brave and trying to intervene in a Bully Beat Down. That also never ended well for the teacher or the pupil; teachers who intervened would come into school the next day beaten up, bruised and battered. This was not lost on the other teachers.

Things would go back to the way they were. The unfortunate child who tried to save or assist anyone getting their Bully Beat Down would themselves be bullied that much worse the following day. Kids would never try to help again, in fear of what the next level of punishment would be. Lessons were learned.

In the classroom, the Vietnamese kids sat on benches near the front. From there they could learn better; they could hear the teacher more clearly and actually see what was going on. The Chinese kids sat behind them; they were the runts of the litter - the lowest of the low. Even sitting just a few feet back from the front made it difficult to hear or see what was going on.

The Chinese didn't learn much, if anything. That continued until they were abused enough to leave the province or, better yet, the country. Hung, being a Half-Breed, was put in the far back right corner where seeing the teacher was impossible and hearing anything that the teacher might be saying was only possible occasionally. Even at nine years old, Hung couldn't really read or write. Both his speech and his command of the Vietnamese language was considered only just about understandable at best.

LITTLE DRAGON

Since Hung sat at the back of the room, when break time came around, he was always able to sneak out of the building quickly: the first out of his classroom. It was made easier for him since the adults didn't pay much attention to a Half-Breed anyway.

He would high-tail it out from the back of the school, rushing to the top of a small nearby hill which the kids called I-Cee hill; where there lived an old lady in a small hut. The little old lady worked as a domestic help in the home of a wealthy family in another part of the town. She would "liberate" chunks of ice from her employers' freezers. Arriving home with the ice, she took a sweet-tasting coloring which she had made from crushed plants and froze it into ice cubes which she broke off the large lumps that she had taken, before selling the sweetened ice to anyone for whatever sum the buyers could muster. This was a treat, especially since Vietnam's heat could dry the saliva in your mouth before you could swallow your spit.

As he got older, being on the streets taught Hung a thing or two about hustling. He learned fast how to make a quick buck. His favorite hang-out was a place - a den - where men and women drank and gambled, wasting their time away and losing their money. Gambling and drinking made them need a fetcher - a runner, usually just a kid, who would steal what the adults wanted and sell it on to them.

Hung would steal packs of cigarettes from the local market to take to his customers at the gambling den. Since the gamblers always wanted to stay there in the hope of luck and fortune, leaving the gambling tables or their winnings was not an option. Hung's hustling skills automatically kicked into a business operation. He could sell a single smoke to the gamblers in the den for double the market price - usually the local brand of long, thin, black cigarettes - the 555. He would do all kinds of odd jobs for the gamblers, like fetching booze, food or water. Whatever anyone wanted, Hung got it for them for any coin he could get. It seemed as if he was never at home: he had become **Bụi Đời** - homeless... **a street urchin**.

Hung and the other children on the streets couldn't afford the cigarettes that he was selling. He couldn't afford tobacco. He didn't even smoke one of the stolen cigarettes; that would reduce his takings. When he had the chance, however, he and the other kids would try *thuốc lào*, smoked through a *điếu cày* - a water pipe - made from a piece of bamboo cane. When the water in the pipe needed to be topped up, the kids were usually too high on *thuốc lào* to get more water: instead, one of them would piss in the pipe to bring it back up to the required level. By that stage, they were too far gone to notice any difference in what they were smoking. The *thuốc lào* was - and is - incredibly strong and has powerful side effects on users. It can be up to one thousand times stronger than tobacco and so Hung could only smoke it in small doses: it would have blown Hung's socks off - if he had had any socks.

Throughout his childhood, Hung smoked *thuốc lào* whenever he could, even though after a few puffs, he found that he got the shakes and his body would start to tremble. Sometimes he would even froth at the mouth - white foam would bubble out between his lips and run down to his chin. When that happened, he usually went into a deep trance: awake but not awake at the same time. He would have to be slapped about the face, hard, to bring him round and back to consciousness. His body developed a degree of tolerance to the power of *thuốc lào*: gradually he was able to endure its strength.

All the running away from bullies and gangs had made Hung a really fast runner and the local gamblers liked him for it. His hustling didn't earn him much, but when you're running around all day so that you don't have time to spend anything and when you have no other possessions, then if you can get a few coins, even just one or two feels like a lot.

Another bonus from the hustling: when Hung ran up the hill to visit the hut lady, he had his own money to pay for a delicious, cold, sweet ice. Hung would bring a small cloth with him in which to wrap the ice, to slow down the melting in the intense heat.

Hung started noticing that other boys were following him to see the lady and to get some fresh cold ice. He always made sure to be there first, because sometimes the hut lady would run out. Unfortunately, on this blazing hot day, just when he thought nothing could stop him from enjoying some nice cold ice cubes, the hut lady ran out of ice. One of the larger kids kicked off big time: he was furious when the hut lady announced that she was out of supplies.

The kid's rage brought out in him a big flaw in his character which Hung was all too familiar with. Hung watched while the big kid turned into a bully, using his size to get what he wanted. The bully walked over to the smallest kid who had already enjoying his cold afternoon treat and snatched the boy's ice cubes. He then kicked the boy to the ground.

Hung thought to himself: *"At least it's not me this time."*

But inside his stomach, something was telling him different. Something - or someone - was nagging at him that this wasn't right. This new force - a gut feeling - was telling Hung that finally, he had had enough. Enough of the demons inside him and enough of the bullying. Who protects the weak?

"Is this my life from here on in? Forever?" he wondered to himself.

Hung felt the demons start releasing their grip on his guts. As he clenched his fists tightly, he started to feel an inner warmth deep inside his body. He could feel his teeth grinding together, harder and harder, while he watched the bully laughing and spitting sweet-water in the little boy's face.

Hung moved closer toward the little boy on the ground. He tried to stop himself and began questioning his own sanity, but still he kept moving forward. He knew this wasn't going to end well, no matter what happened. His head seemed to be shouting at him, time after time: "STOP!" - but he kept going all the same.

Hung walked up to the little boy and offered him a helping hand. He tightened his grip around the large ice cube he had just bought from the hut lady. As he squeezed it, he could feel the coldness through the cloth. Hung noticed the bully out of the corner of his eye. The bully was pulling his arm back and squeezing his fist to come down hard on Hung, but it ended up being a fake punch. This bully wasn't skilled in street fighting like Hung. With a quick shift of his weight to his rear leg, Hung twisted his body and jabbed his ice-filled fist upwards onto the bully's chin.

Hung could feel the ice crumble under the pressure of his blows to the bully's face. The bones in his knuckles screamed.

LITTLE DRAGON

The swellings over the bully's eyes started to make his vision blurred and fuzzy. The bully's neck whipped back and a few teeth sprayed across the ground, along with a piece of his tongue; one of Hung's punches had hit the boy square on the chin while his mouth was open. The force of the punch snapped the bully's teeth together violently, so that part of his tongue was chopped off.

The bully covered his mouth in confusion. He couldn't believe what was happening to him. The ringing in his head caused him to stumble back a few steps before he started to recover his bearings. He shook his head a few times and spat out a mouthful of blood, along with another tooth. Hung watched him feel inside his mouth with a finger, finding the gaping hole where once had been his front teeth.

The bully tried to focus his eyes and then stared at Hung with a look with which Hung was already familiar. The boy was really seeing red now: without a second thought, he launched himself like a runaway train, straight in Hung's direction.

He slammed his shoulder into Hung's chest. The air left Hung's lungs in a whoosh. The bully's shoulder had smashed Hung's hands into his chest, increasing massively the pressure on his ribs. The bigger boy's extra weight magnified the concussion from the blow. Hung was blasted backwards off his feet.

Hung's back slammed hard onto the ground, causing him immediately to start gasping for air. His chest heaved from trying to drag oxygen back into his lungs. Hung rolled over onto his hands, just as the bully was rushing in with a kick to Hung's stomach to continue the onslaught. The bully's kick slammed his foot hard onto Hung's back. Hung was smashed back onto the ground again, directly onto his face.

"You're going to pay with your life, you little shit!" said the thug. Hung smirked as he heard the lisping words whistling through the new gaps in the bully's teeth.

The bully grabbed Hung by the back of his neck, raising his head off the ground, then slammed him back into the dirt. A flash blinded Hung's vision as his brain rattled inside his skull, almost causing him to black out. One of Hung's arms was forced under his chest, between his body and the ground, crushing two of his fingers.

When the side of his face smashed into the ground, the pain seared through the rest of his body. He tasted the blood that was filling his mouth and a couple of his teeth felt loose. A sense of desperation filled Hung's consciousness and his fear demon started to rear its head again, taking control of his thoughts. This boy was going to kill him.

Hung felt his head pulled back up one more time. It was going to be smashed down hard. He pushed his arms up under his chest, forcing himself upwards quickly and violently. Putting his body under the most extreme pressure and trying to ignore the pain, Hung twisted the upper half of his body - his arms, shoulders and torso - and spun his elbow back. The hard point of his elbow smashed directly into his target's throat, crushing his attacker's larynx into the back of his neck.

With the bully's voice box fractured, his scream of agony was cut short. The bully fell to the ground with a loud thud, squirming like a wounded animal. A great feeling of anger surfaced in Hung. He sat on a dirt mound, frowning and spitting out blood. He allowed himself another smirk while he watched adults suddenly appear out of nowhere. Where

LITTLE DRAGON

were they when he needed them? They rushed to help the defeated, beaten-up bully. No one came to help him.

CHAPTER FIVE

The intense sweltering heat of the morning woke up Hung. He was drenched in sweat. His face was still a little tender, even a week after the last big fight, but at least his skin was healing well. Severe nerve damage from numerous previous beatings and attacks had taken a lot of feeling from the side of his face, but Hung thought of this as helpful since he would no longer be able to feel pain so much.

Hung threw on his clothes as fast as he could before rushing outside. As usual, his mother was already gone for the day, but that was a good thing because after the last big school fight (which the local kids began referring to as the "Viet Cong School Riots") she had become even meaner than ever. Her punishments became more severe and painful, although Hung felt he didn't deserve them. However, he was beginning to worry that she was losing control of herself altogether because of everything they were going through; she just seemed to be getting worse, ever since his father and brother had left them that day so long ago. How long was it now? Nearly three years? Hung was starting to forget what his father looked or sounded like. And it would be worse for Quân: he would remember nothing.

But in Hung's mind "Today Will Be a Great Day!" He was ready to find out the surprise that his friends were going to tell him about - the one that the twins had mentioned before Hung had been beaten up. They didn't want to tell him while he was still in a lot of pain and black and blue with bruises; they wanted to wait until he was well on the way to recovery.

They told him that he needed to be in tip-top shape to enjoy this particular surprise so he'd better be ready. And Hung was ready. He was far stronger than before and he was up for anything.

Hung started his morning by running over to meet up with his friends at the old factory near his village. The factory was fairly close to his home so it didn't take long for him to get there. It was also close to the sea, on the banks of the estuary where the nearby river turned tidal and salty before it drained its flow into the sea. Tranh and Duong had stumbled across their surprise for Hung late one evening at low tide, completely by chance. They had been watching boats at anchor in the river estuary: the boats were waiting for the tide to come in so that they could enter the harbor, ready to load and unload cargo.

He saw his friends waiting on a mound a few hundred feet away from the factory. The factory was old and the majority of its construction had been from recycled metals. It had never been attractive to look at but now it was even worse: the rusting metal finish gave the factory an evil, dark, look - as if it contained hidden secrets.

"Hey, it's Hamburger Face!" Tranh yelled out when he saw Hung approaching.

Hung's two friends had light fingers and they had nicked a couple of snacks to eat on the way to the factory. As a matter of fact, Duong had taught Hung about nicking. Duong was the best pickpocket thief that Hung had ever seen.

LITTLE DRAGON

"Hey, guys," Hung called out as he walked up to greet his new brothers. Duong looked at Hung and was startled: there was something unusual and rather peculiar about Hung that day: he was smiling. Hung hadn't smiled in a long time and Duong barely recognized him when he did it.

Duong tore off a chunk of the bread he had stolen and threw it to Hung. He knew Hung ate a lot less than they did and they barely ate at all! Hung caught the bread in mid-air and gave Duong a grateful nod.

"So what's the big secret?" Hung asked, with his mouth stuffed from the big wedge of bread he was in the process of gobbling down.

"Tranh saw them bringing stuff inside here," Duong told him, pointing at the factory.

"OK..." Hung said, drawing out as much sarcasm as he could squeeze from a single word. "Congratulations." He mocked them with a smirk and a shrug of his shoulders.

"You dork," Tranh said, smacking Hung on his shoulder. "We've a chance to nick some cool stuff from there."

"Do you know what kind of stuff?" Hung asked. He had his doubts: the factory was old and run-down so he assumed that what was inside it would be the same.

"Yeah!" Duong immediately told him, with great excitement in his voice. "The valuable kind!"

Hung rolled his eyes: he had been expecting that kind of answer. The three of them jogged along the track, closer to the old factory, to see if they could discover a bit more about what was going on there. Although there were not many of them, Hung noticed that there were at least two guards posted around the factory perimeter.

He couldn't afford to get into trouble again: his own mother might consider finishing him off for good if he got caught up in anything. Hung posed a question to his partners in crime.

"Have either of you geniuses thought about how we're getting in there?"

"Of course," Tranh told him. "Who d'you think the brains of this operation is?"

"Ohh! I was unaware that brains were a part of this operation. I thought it was just you and your brother," Hung teased them, but with a laugh.

Tranh and Duong laughed with Hung. "Follow us, smartass!" Duong said, beckoning Hung over to him with a wave of his hand.

The three of them set off again towards the shoreline, keeping close to the factory's security fence. They could hear the sound of the waves rolling onto the shore: they were close to the sea now. The grass under their feet changed color. There were also long strands of seaweed which had been washed up by the waves during storms.

There was only one guard patrolling this section of the perimeter, so they made their way away from the security fence to avoid being seen. There were other guards stationed at the entrance doors to the factory. The guards were talking amongst themselves, taking little notice of what was going on around them. Some were sitting at a nearby table having a break. They were playing cards and smoking. All of them were doing anything but paying attention to maintaining security at the factory. Hung, Tranh and Duong crept past another gate guard who had fallen asleep while he had been reading pornographic magazines. Then they tiptoed back to the perimeter fence at the quietest point they could find, out of sight of all the guards.

They climbed over the fence and scrambled down a steep earth bank that led to a small drop onto a sandbar on the bank of the river where it ran alongside the factory. It was low tide so it was necessary to slide down about ten feet.

The smell of the sea entered Hung's nose and the familiar sounds of the shore reached his ears. There were many crabs stuck in the fallen trees that were a particular feature of the tidal estuary at this point: it would be a great idea to remember to grab a few crabs on the way home to surprise his mother with some tasty treats for dinner.

"So the big surprise is a night of crabbing as the sun sets?" he asked. "I'm sure you guys might consider this romantic and all, but you really aren't my type. No offence!" he teased them, holding his hand to his chest, like a bad theater actor, trying to show that his character was in love.

Duong laughed and shook his head. "Where do you come up with all this stuff, drama queen?" Duong asked him.

"I'm just naturally fantastic this way," Hung responded. He looked smug.

Hung watched Tranh cross the damp bank of sand to the edge of the water where he had previously tied a rowing boat to one of the fallen trees that rested half in, half out of the river.

LITTLE DRAGON

He picked carefully where he put his feet, walking only on rocks and branches from fallen trees; some of the sand was very soft and it was easy to sink into it and get stuck. Duong followed close behind, imitating Tranh and being careful not to fall into the murky water of the river or get his feet sucked in by the sand.

"Never put your feet on the sand during low tide," Tranh told Hung. "Your legs are sure to get stuck and that'll be really bad when the tide comes back in."

Hung followed their lead, crossing over to the boat. All three of them climbed in. Tranh and Duong grabbed the oars and cast off while Hung sat in the middle, watching.

"Anyone want to reveal this big secret before I really start freaking out?" Hung begged them to tell him what was going on as they drifted closer and closer toward the basement level of the gigantic scary factory.

"Awww, is little Hung getting scared?" Duong cracked out, trying to mock Hung while at the same time attempting, unsuccessfully to mask the shakiness in his own voice.

"Last time me and Duong were pulling some crabs off the trees, we accidentally drifted very close to the factory but then we noticed something," Tranh told him. By now, the three boys were floating slowly past a large iron pillar.

"There!" Duong said, pointing to the right, just after they were completely past the pillar.

Hung noticed, deep under the main floor of the factory, there was a secret entrance - an opening out into the river, a bit like a cave. No one could get to the entrance while the tide was high and it was concealed from anyone who was snooping around when the tide was low. It was well hidden by a natural barrier of fallen, rotting, trees and other vegetation that had washed down the river and become tangled up in the dead trees.

"What's in there?" Hung asked, suspecting that they had already taken a look inside.

"We haven't gone in yet," Tranh responded.

Duong chimed in: "We wanted to wait for you, of course."

Hung felt a sense of joy and pride running through him. He knew he couldn't find better friends than the ones he had: he felt that they were a team.

"Well, let's raid it then!" Hung suggested.

Tranh and Duong paddled up to the opening, preparing to scramble up off the boat. Tranh climbed up to the entrance as quietly as possible with his two brothers-in-arms close behind, just in case there was anyone watching - or anyone inside the passageway which they could now see ran into the rocks, under the factory. By this time, daylight was almost gone and the under-belly of the factory was getting quite dark.

Of course, none of them had thought about bringing anything capable of producing light: no torches or matches. They crept through the entrance and into the passage, heading closer to what looked like a door at its end. Once they were close enough, they saw that it was actually a heavy iron gate with a big old rusted lock that looked so old that it could have been made before the first wheel.

"Nice one," Hung added. "Does anyone have the key?" he asked.

"Dammit!" Tranh said, kicking the gate with the ball of his foot.

The gate shook off a large cloud of rusty dust then let out a scary metal groan before slowly falling over with a loud "clang", which echoed back and forward in the corridor for several seconds. The three of them jumped in surprise, tripping over and bumping into one another.

They darted away into the shadows, trying to look for places to hide, only to realize that there weren't any. After a few moments, however, they noticed that the racket they had made appeared not to have attracted the attention of the guards. They stopped and stared … at the passageway in front of them - waiting to see if anyone would come.

They waited still longer Nothing else happened. No one appeared. There was no gunfire, shouting or anything else. Hung swatted Tranh on the back of the head, quite hard.

Tranh frowned and sulked, rubbing where Hung had clobbered him. He turned toward Hung, looking at him angrily. Hung stared at him, signaling by his glare that another slap was about to come across his face if he had anything else to say.

"Like I knew that was going to happen!" Tranh hissed.

"And you're supposed to be the brains of the operation - right?" Hung asked. He couldn't keep a tone of sarcasm out of his voice.

"Yeah, well... '" Tranh responded.

Duong headed back towards the fallen gate to check if the coast was still clear. He couldn't hear or see anyone, although at this point nobody could see much of anything; it was too dark.

Duong scrambled back to them, reporting back. "Looks OK to me," he told them.

Slowly they started to make their way along the corridor on the other side of the gate, groping around in the gloom for a while - until they noticed a small room off to one side. By now, they were just about working by touch alone. The room led to a small door that was in front of a staircase, heading upwards, but the natural light they had been relying upon from outside to see what was going on wasn't going to last much longer so they didn't go any further.

"Look over there in the corner," Hung whispered.

They hurried over to the corner, where they found a small stack of cloth packets. They were not very heavy: they looked a bit like small backpacks, but without the straps. The boys quickly grabbed some of the packets, two each, and headed back along the passageway, into the darkness and back to the boat.

As the band of brothers headed outside again, they joshed and cracked jokes, laughing at each other as they slipped and slid on the slimy metallic floor of the corridor. The sun was gone for the day and the moon was on the rise but it provided minimal light. The three friends each took an oar and paddled their boat back up the river, until they were a good distance away from the factory, at which point they

LITTLE DRAGON

beached the boat and tied it off on a tree. Each of them picked up two of the packs they had taken from the factory and headed up the hill to check out their treasure.

"Let's take a look," Tranh said, his greedy eyes trying to pull at the knots around one of the packets faster than his hands could untie them. Opening it up, he found that there were various pockets or sections inside.

Suddenly, his smile vanished as he pulled out of one of the pockets a square piece of whitish gray clay - the like of which he had never seen before. With a confused look on his face, he set the clay on the ground and opened up another pocket of the pack, this time taking out a small silver-colored metallic cylinder with some lengths of a cloth-like material coiled around it. The coils were of different lengths, held in place by a loop in one of the coils.

"What the hell is this stuff?" Duong queried, pulling out the same things from his pack as Tranh had.

"Fuck if I know," Hung answered, equally puzzled.

"It's used to make bombs," a voice from behind whispered softly to them.

The boys leapt up, all squealing in surprise and turning to face the voice that frightened them. Looming behind them was an older boy, probably in his mid-teens, although Hung couldn't really tell. He was a big guy, standing there with his arms crossed and the start of a smirk on his face.

"Bombs?" asked Tranh, his voice quivering a little.

"Yup, they use it for blasting in the mountains over that-away." The teenager pointed towards the top of a nearby hill. "It's hard for them to dig through the rocks up there so they use this stuff and just blast through it."

Hung wasn't sure what to make of this guy. He was suspicious - but his curiosity got the better of him.

"Oh yeah…?? Well, first off, who the fuck are you? Second: piss off for scaring the hell out of us. And how do you know all this?" Hung asked.

"I'm Xiang and my dad used to work up there until about a month ago," Xiang told them.

"What happened to him? Did they shut down the factory?" Duong asked. "No," Xiang replied. "He died in an electrical explosion... an accident," Xiang told him.

"What's an electrical explosion accident?" Tranh asked him.

Xiang looked down towards the ground for a moment. "The gray clay stuff is the stuff that explodes. But it's useless without sticking one of those metal tubes in it. That's the detonator. The length of coil sticking out of the end of the detonator is the fuse. Once you light that, you'd better run!"

"So your dad lit it and didn't run?" Duong asked.

"Worse", Xiang told him. "He was laying out the gray stuff you've got there on the mountainside, in the rain, ready for them to carry out the next explosion, and he got struck by lightning."

The kids' jaws dropped listening to Xiang's story.

"That's not even the worst part," Xiang added.

"How can it get worse than that?" Hung asked.

Xiang continued: "The workers said he was electrocuted from the lightning for a second before the electricity hit the clay stuff and blew him up."

The three boys stood motionless, looking at Xiang staring in disbelief.

"I'm just kidding!" Xiang said with a grin. "He actually died from a heart attack," he told them.

"WHAT!! A heart attack??" Tranh shook his head, no longer believing anything Xiang was telling them.

"Yeah, he was having sex with a prostitute... but my dad was old," Xiang hung his head. Hung laughed and punched Xiang on the shoulder.

"Whatever, man. Now we're supposed to believe your dad died having sex with some bimbo prostitute and had a heart attack. What do you think we are, man? Stupid?"

Xiang looked up at the boys. "That bimbo was my mom, man," he replied.

The boys looked on in shock and puzzlement, bewildered as to whether this was the truth of the story.

"He was my mom's favorite customer," Xiang continued shaking his head. The three boys bust up, laughing their heads off. "Yeah, right!!" Tranh guffawed.

Xiang stood there, still with his head down. "Anyway, you guys might wanna be careful with that clay stuff. I wasn't kidding about it exploding, you know."

While they had been talking with Xiang, a few more kids who obviously knew Xiang and who had overheard the conversation walked over to join the crowd. Xiang shook hands with the kids as they joined the group.

"If you don't believe me, I can show you," he told them. Their eyes lit up like it was Christmas. They had a present and it was time to open it. They had the bomb! One of the last kids to shake Xiang's hand, the largest of them, approached closer. "This is my mate, Butch," Xiang told everyone. Butch was smoking... something or other. It smelt disgusting.

Xiang knelt down, opened one of the packs again and tore off a small chunk from the lump of explosive, then stuck one of the cylinders - the detonator - into it. He put his hand out to Butch, who put into it a dirty, rusty Zip lighter which he had taken from his pocket. Xiang flipped the lighter, lit one of the coils on the end of the detonator and threw the assembled bomb at a tree a short distance away. As he did so, Hung noticed how quickly the flame spread along with the coil

They waited for a few seconds but nothing happened. Butch started to say, "Must have been..."

BOOM! A huge bang, the size of which they had never heard before, rang out into the night with a massively bright flash of light.

Xiang's friends scattered in all directions while Hung and his two friends scooped up the six packs again and ran home as fast as their legs could get them there. As they did so, fragments of the tree floated down from the sky. It had been shredded into tiny pieces. Tranh and Duong both noticed they had pissed their pants from fright. No one said anything that made sense - to themselves, never mind to any of the others. They just screamed all their way home. Each of the boys was, however, on the ball enough to remember to grab the packs of explosives which they had taken from the factory: something was telling them that there was good money to make from the contents of the packs.

Hung rushed home in record-breaking time, he felt he was moving so fast he thought he would never be able to stop.

Once Hung made it home, he was thankful to find out that his mother wasn't back yet. He quickly shoved one of the packs under his sleeping pad where his mother wouldn't see it. He was also careful to make sure that Quân didn't see him hide the pack; he didn't want his little brother playing with it.

The other pack he took a short distance along the road to hide in his back-up secret place. Next, he quickly changed his clothes then put the dirty ones in a pile for cleaning later in the week. Finally, it was time for Hung to get some rest. It had been a busy - and exciting - day.

Early the next morning, he went out to earn some cash from the local gangsters, the gamblers and the early drinkers. There was no school today so Hung's plan was to spend some time nicking and selling things for coin to help out his mother. He headed back home around the middle of the day, eating some food that he'd nicked along the way.

Once home, he checked his hidden stashes. After satisfying himself that they were safe and secure, he headed out again to meet up with his friends at the boat. Tranh and

Duong were already there with a pack each in their hands.

Hung didn't bring his. He thought that carrying too much around like that was just not smart, especially after he saw what it could do. Hung trotted up to his friends.

"Why did you both bring a pack, instead of both of you bringing just one?" Hung asked.

"We... did... both bring one," Duong exclaimed, confused and shaking his head.

They set out in the rowing boat again down the river and into the estuary, past the evil-looking factory. After drifting downstream for about fifteen minutes, they came to a small cove where the estuary widened out.

"This should be a good enough distance," Tranh said to the guys as they anchored.

"So what's the plan?" Hung asked.

"I've come up with an idea, right? Instead of trying to sell this stuff; let's just use it," Tranh suggested.

"OK then, genius. Let's see it," Hung said to Tranh, gesturing him to take the stage.

Tranh took a small piece of clay, setting it up just like Xiang had done the previous night... except that Tranh first pushed a number of small stones and rocks into the clay and next he wrapped the clay and the rocks in several pieces of cloth. It was like a weighted ball, about the size of a fist. He added one of the detonators.

"That should do it," Tranh said, looking pleased with his new creation.

Hung questioned the mighty brain of Tranh. "That should do what?"

"Fishing bomb," Tranh announced.

"A fishing bomb?" Hung asked.

"Yeah, a fishing bomb. We throw the bomb in the water. It explodes, knocking out all the fish. Boom! We win the prize of a huge fish dinner!" Tranh explained, with a big smile. He was proud of his invention and was wanting to boast about the brilliance of his idea.

Hung had big doubts - and was also a bit scared - but if it worked, that would be a lot of fish. He went against his better judgment: "OK, Tranh. Your plan sounds like it should work."

"What the hell," Duong said with a sigh. "Let's give it a try."

Tranh pulled out a box of matches from his pocket and struck one. Everyone looked quickly at each other. Then with a shaky hand, Tranh lit the coil, the fuse for the detonator. It sparked and the flame raced along like it a snake.

In haste, Tranh threw it overboard, away from the boat, as far as he could. The bomb made a small splash as it hit the water. It floated for less than a second, then sank. They could see the fuse sparkling under the water for a bit longer before it sank out of sight. Then... Nothing. Silence.

"Dammit!" Duong shouted in disappointment. Suddenly, they felt a series of waves, pulses of strong vibrations hitting the bottom of their boat. Seconds later, a few bubbles burst out of the surface of the water. The boys leaned back into the boat just in time, just before a vast balloon of spray and fish guts broke through the surface and exploded into the air. It rained fish guts for a few seconds. By the time it stopped, most of the boat and all three boys were pretty much covered in bloody gore - and they were all soaked.

"Didn't see that coming!" Tranh said with huge understatement.

Hung and Duong looked at him - then they all burst out into hysterical laughter.

When they had recovered from their laughter, the boys started scanning the surface of the water, sifting through all the floating parts. Overall, they managed to find about a dozen fish that were edible among the huge number of totally destroyed ones.

Duong giggled. "Guess we should move a bit further along. I don't think the rest of the fish are going to stick around for the next fireworks show."

"Good call," Hung replied.

The boys continued with their fishing bonanza for several hours until they had a large enough quantity of fish to take back to Tranh's and Duong's house. They planned to store it over the next several days to eat until it went bad. Then they would go back to stock up again. With the amount of explosives they had taken from the factory, they now had the means to allow them to feed their families for several months if it was done right.

LITTLE DRAGON

When they finished, they paddled back upstream and beached the boat.

Tranh grabbed a large bag of fish and a smaller one of larger pieces of fish while the other two boys each took a small sack filled with enough fish to last a few days. They said their goodbyes and headed home.

CHAPTER SIX

Hung was very pleased with himself. "I've had an idea," he said as he, Tranh and Duong wandered slowly along the road back from school one afternoon, a few days later.

"Careful. You might hurt yourself, Hung. You know that you overheat when you do something reckless like thinking!" Tranh teased him.

"Yeah, yeah. Very funny," said Hung. "If you're going to be like that, I won't tell you, but before you take the piss out of me again, the idea I have is a way that I can get back at Psycho and his gang. You two have had the shit beaten out of you by Psycho too. Of course, if you aren't interested... Or if you are too sissy..." Hung tailed off, hoping that he had made the twins curious enough to ask for more. He had.

"OK. I'll bite," said Duong. "I expect I'll regret it, but if you want to yap at us, we'll listen."

Hung paused for effect and then said, "We know what the explosives and detonators can do. I reckon that the detonators by themselves are fucking awesome. You hardly need to put the explosives with them as well. All I want to do is to scare the shit out of Psycho and the psychos, not kill them. That might be hard to explain!"

LITTLE DRAGON

"Get on with it!, said Tranh, sounding rather impatient. "If you've got an idea, then tell us".

"All right. All right," said Hung. "You know Old Phuoc's yard? That's where we could set them up."

Old Phuoc was a stallholder in the market, trying to sell what he said was "fresh" meat - pork from the pigs that he kept at home. He usually killed a pig every week or so, but as he was almost always grumpy and bad-tempered - and charged too much for his meat - he didn't sell much and people went to other stalls. His wife kept about forty or so chickens, mainly in cages, and the eggs that they didn't need were sold alongside the meat - with greater success.

His other main failing was hygiene: he stank of pig shit all day, every day. He never seemed to wash. He kept his pigs in filthy conditions: mud and muck all over the place. It was impossible to see the color of the pigs in the backyard of his run-down house: they were always caked in mud and their own shit.

The pig-pens were rarely cleaned out. It was usually only done when neighbors complained, first to Old Phuoc and then to the authorities about the disgusting smell and the flies. Then, reluctantly, Old Phuoc would shovel the pig shit out of the enclosures and pile it up into a huge heap at the entrance to his yard, immediately next to the narrow path that ran past the front of his house. The heap never seemed to get smaller: it grew throughout the year until once in a while - a long while - the rest of the village would get together, collect up as much of the muck heap as they could and cart it away, to spread on the fields.

His wife was more energetic about cleaning out the

chickens: she did this regularly but she then added the chicken poo to the pig shit heap. Chicken shit is worse than pig shit in many ways: the mixture of smells was overpowering and nauseous.

Old Phuoc made matters worse: when the pig and chicken shit was piled up and had started to rot, liquid manure would run out of the bottom of the heap. For a time it spread across Old Phuoc's garden - and his vegetables grew well as a result. However, when the liquid shit started to run into his house, his wife kicked up a fuss. Old Phuoc, therefore, dug a trench, about half a meter deep, beside the muck heap, between the house and the heap. That soon filled with powerful-smelling liquid shit and so his wife would use buckets to scoop it out and spread it on their vegetable garden. It was lethal stuff if inhaled for too long.

The only good thing was that Old Phuoc's house was, in effect, at the end of the path. The path went a bit further, down to an abandoned pond which was, now and then, used for washing animals, but it was very rare for anyone other than Old Phuoc to go further along the path, beyond his house. The rumor was that he went there to get drinking water for himself and his wife as the water supply to their place was so polluted by the pig shit.

Opposite Old Phuoc's place was thick jungle, which came right up to the pathway: you needed a machete to hack your way into it. The nearest neighbors were about thirty meters further up the path, towards the road.

Duong and Tranh were definitely very interested. What had Hung got in mind? How would Old Phuoc's yard help Hung get back at Psycho and the gang? Hung read their minds.

"We will need to prepare for it. First, we need to block off the pathway beyond Old Phuoc's place so that Psycho and the rest can't go further down that way. We also need to block the path somehow behind Psycho, once we have got him and his gang down to Old Phuoc's place, just in case. We'll never have another chance. Some fencing panels, tied up to the trees, which we can cut down to fall onto the path should do it. Timing will be everything."

Hung then explained his idea in more detail. The others grew excited. Yes, it had risks. It could go horribly wrong, but if it came off... It would be fantastic! It was worth a go, they reckoned. However, Hung didn't want to appear too keen: he was determined to appear "cool", although inside he was quivering with excitement, particularly now that the twins were on side with him.

It took about a week of planning, rehearsals and preparation but eventually, they were ready. The main delay had been getting hold of the bamboo fencing panels. Fortunately, another stallholder nearby took down a section of five panels from around his yard, in order to carry out some repairs to them. He left them stacked neatly in his front yard, ready for his attention. They "disappeared" from his yard the first night, only to be found again after Hung had taken his revenge. A sharp knife was borrowed from the kitchen at the twins' home and a length of thin rope was "liberated" from the back of someone's motorbike. A Zip lighter was pick pocketed easily during a busy time in the marketplace. Hung had schooled the twins until they were bored stiff with the story they were to spin. The story intended for Psycho and his gang - and

LITTLE DRAGON

them only - to hear.

Timing would be everything. They chose a time when Old Phuoc and his wife would be at the market; Old Phuoc trying vainly to sell his vomit-making meat and the slightly better eggs and his wife yapping with her friends. The path down to Old Phuoc's place should be deserted.

The first job was to block off the path where it went beyond Old Phuoc's house down to the pond. This was done by breaking off some branches from nearby trees and jamming them at different heights across the path. A few enormous banana tree leaves concealed the torn-off ends.

After a big struggle, the three boys eventually managed to drag the five fence panels down the path, one at a time, then prop them up so that the base of each of them rested on the ground on the opposite side of the path, just before the path passed in front of Old Phuoc's place. The panels were then pushed upright, one by one so that they stood vertically side by side, parallel to the path. Tranh took the rope with him and, with help from the others, clambered up a tree which stood behind the panels, also on the opposite side of the path to Old Phuoc's house.

Tranh flipped the rope around a branch of the tree, then he tied the panel that was closest to the path onto the rope. The other four panels were trapped between the tree and the first panel. He loosened off the rope a little so that the panels tipped down a little towards the path. If the rope holding the first panel should be removed, all five panels would fall across the path, so that some of them would land on top of the fence belonging to Old Phuoc's neighbor. Some of the panels were just a bit taller than the path was wide and they were all of the slightly different lengths: the boys had made sure that the shorter ones were stacked standing straight up, closest to the path. Again, banana tree leaves were used to cover the panels on the side that faced onto the path.

The hope was that Psycho and his friends wouldn't notice the panels in their excitement. The panels had a two-fold function: to slow up the retreat of the gang back along the path should they smell a rat before Hung's trap was sprung and also to stop Old Phuoc or anyone else coming along the path while the boys were springing their surprise upon Psycho. The boys didn't want anyone other than Psycho and the gang to be the targets.

That left one thing to do. Hung dug out one of the detonators from the packs he had taken from the factory. Their experience with the Fishing Bombs had given them some idea how fast the fuses burnt once they had been lit. He also knew that for what he planned, he would not need any of the explosives. That would be too much. He cut off what he thought would be the right length and ensured that it was attached firmly to the detonator. He reckoned two minutes would be enough. Carefully he pushed the detonator into the middle of the muck heap with one hand, pushing in as far as his arm would go - up to the armpit. With the fingers of his other hand he was pinching his nose tightly: the foul stink was terrible. Hung felt quite ill and was sure that he was going to throw up any minute. Even repeated vigorous scrubbing sessions in the local pond later would not shift all of the stench that was now, it seemed, lodged forever in his arm. There remained a certain "aroma" for about a week afterwards.

The time had come... Hung checked the marketplace. Yes: Old Phuoc and his wife were both there. There would be no one at their home. He nodded to Tranh and Duong:

they were ready... Hung left them to it. He ran back to Old Phuoc's house.

"Have you heard?" asked Tranh to Duong in a loud whisper. "It's a big secret. Swear you won't tell anyone. Old Phuoc has a fortune in gold hidden in that shit heap in his front yard."

"Fuck off", said Duong in disbelief. "How d'you know?"

"I know, that's all," said Tranh, getting more theatrical with his whispers. "Old Phuoc doesn't spend a cent if he can avoid it. He lives in the shit of his pigs and doesn't buy anything. He even gets his wife to sew rags together for him for his clothes. He must have masses of cash that he is sitting on. Anyway, I was down the path past his place this morning and I saw him hiding something in the shit heap. He was on the other side of the heap, nearest the house. He was standing between the shit heap and that horrible trench full of... Liquid shit. He looked about him to make sure no one was looking, then he went up to the heap and shoved four or five packages into the heap on that side of it. He didn't see me: he's getting blind. I was able to get up close and hid behind his handcart to watch him. What else would he be putting into the shit heap? Even he wouldn't shove his hand into it without a good reason. What better place to hide things than a disgusting place like that?"

"Huh. Still don't believe you," said Duong, playing his part to perfection.

Tranh shrugged his shoulders. "I'm going to have a look.

LITTLE DRAGON

Apart from trying not to throw up from the stench, I've nothing to lose. Need to do it now: there's talk that the neighbors are pissed off again by the flies and maggots coming from the shit heap so they are going to start clearing it tomorrow. Don't know if Old Phuoc knows that, so he may lose whatever's there".

"Waste of time," Duong said, dismissively. I'm not going to end up stinking like a sewer."

"Up to you, Shit for Brains", retorted Tranh. "I'm going down there now, as soon as I've had some food. I'm starving. Let's nick some noodles off Diep's stall and then go and check out the heap. Unless of course, you have something better to do...?"

Tranh left the question hanging. It wasn't aimed at Duong: he had only started talking about what might be in the muck heap when they had sidled up behind Psycho and one of his enforcers who had been sitting on a wall overlooking the market, throwing stones at a couple of small Chinese children who had been playing nearby.

Tranh and Duong hoped that their stage whispers had carried to the cloth ears of Psycho. It wouldn't take long to find out. One thing that Psycho was known for was his enthusiasm to get his hands on the money of others. Giving him the window of opportunity to go straight down to Old Phuoc's place while the twins were supposed to be filling themselves up with noodles was the plan.

Hung would have liked to have spun the story to Psycho himself, but as Duong pointed out, Psycho had it in for Hung and if he had heard Hung's voice, the chances were that Psycho either wouldn't believe Hung and see the trap they were setting, or he would switch off trying to eavesdrop on the conversation and would be after Hung with a knife in his hand.

The twins therefore had to be the ones who set the trap. Hung would spring it.

Sure enough, as Tranh and Duong moved away from the wall, Psycho climbed down. He immediately set off across the marketplace, gathering his gang - nine more of them - from various stalls around the market as he did so. The twins, after making sure that Psycho wasn't looking out for them, set off for Old Phuoc's place like scared rabbits: they ran flat out, as fast as they could, down the path, stopping short of Old Phuoc's fence. They then pushed their way into the bushes growing along the edge of the jungle, on the opposite side of the path, alongside the fencing panels that had been tied up to the tree. Tranh had the sharp knife with him.

They were just in time. A few seconds later, Psycho and his gang appeared further back along the path, walking briskly towards them. The twins crouched down, moving backwards into the bushes, pulling low-hanging tree branches between them and the path to provide some cover. The gang walked past, without seeing them, and entered the front yard of Old Phuoc's property.

Psycho and the gang were not known for going about their activities quietly. They were no different this time. Psycho, of course, was in charge. He directed who searched where. Psycho had remembered well what Tranh had been saying in the marketplace: Psycho and all except one of the gang immediately went around the back of the muck heap, to the side closest to the house. They inched their way along the narrow gap between it and the foul smelling trench which, Hung and the twins had noticed with glee, was full to overflowing. There was some reluctance on the part of most of the gang to shove their hands into the disgusting, stinking, shit heap.

Naturally, they hadn't thought to bring any gloves or tools. Nor did it occur to them to use sticks to poke into the heap. It was bare hands or nothing. Psycho didn't lower himself to put his hands into the pile; he was going to give the orders - which he did, accompanied by shouts and much swearing and punching of gang members if he thought they hadn't put their hands into the heap far enough.

Everyone had an opinion about how the shit heap should be searched - and they all announced their views as loudly as they could. The racket that Psycho and the other thugs were making was sufficient - almost - to cover up entirely the sound of the fence panels falling across the path behind them: as the gang had shuffled around behind the shit heap to start their search, Tranh had cut the rope which was holding up the leaning panels, which fell across the path. The panels which fell first dropped the furthest: none hit the ground but the first one caught on a lower rail of the neighbor's fence near its corner with Old Phuoc's front yard, about ten inches above the surface of the path. The others caught on higher rails of the fence, with the last two, the longest panels, coming to rest on the top rail. Between them, the panels were blocking the path to a height of about five feet.

Hung watched the goings-on with amusement. As the twins had run flat out down the path towards him, Hung had stood on the path and, using the Zip lighter, lit the fuse coil on the detonator. He had lost count how many times he had previously checked and rechecked the lighter to make sure it had fuel and would light. Dozens. Of course, when it came to it, the lighter wasn't the problem: Hung's hands were shaking so much with excitement - and fear - that he nearly dropped the lighter twice and had difficulty flicking it. However, a deep breath and counting to eight helped. Then the fuse caught. Two minutes…

Hung rushed into the front yard of Old Phuoc's property and over to the side wall of the house, furthest away from the muck heap. Not much of a hiding place but it would have to do. Just in time too: as he got there, Psycho and the gang had appeared, coming along the path. They hadn't seen him.

The sound of the falling panels was, however, heard by one of the gang. He was not very smart - certainly not the sharpest knife in the box - and it took a few seconds for him to register in his thick head that something was odd. He was also not the keenest member of the gang; he was along for the ride.

So when the panels fell and he realized that all was not as it should be, he didn't call out to the others, but ran back up the path to the panels and started, in vain, to try and push himself underneath them. He got about halfway when he found himself stuck. He began to wriggle which was the worst thing he could do: that was enough to dislodge the higher panels from where they had been resting on the neighbor's fence so they all fell on top of him, squashing him into the puddles on the path. Thanks to seepage of the raw sewage from the muck heap, it wasn't water in the puddles. The thug's face was pushed down into the stinking liquid. He was lucky, however: he could still breathe - just.

Meanwhile, Psycho's gang were pushing and pulling their hands in and out of the muck heap. It was starting to look like a sieve. Hung's heart was in his mouth. Had the fuse gone out? Was the detonator a dud? Had he miscalculated the timing? Two minutes was taking a lifetime.

"Oh FUCK!!" he thought to himself. *"It hasn't worked. SHIT!!"*

Just as he thought that...

Shit! Huge quantities of shit started flying out in all directions, towards the house, towards the jungle on the other side of the path - and towards Psycho and the gang. A lot went up about forty feet into the air. Solids and liquids. A wide area turned a dark brown, with streaks of yellow, white - from the chicken shit - and many other colors.

However, most of the force went outwards, not upwards: Hung had spoken to Xiang a few days before and picked up ideas about how to position the detonator so that the majority of the shit flew sideways, directly at the gang. Not that Hung had let on to Xiang what he had in mind: the chat with Xiang had been more like "Do you put the detonator in the middle of what you are wanting to blow up, or around the edges of it...?"

Anyone who had been passing by on the path at that moment would have been covered - but no one was. Some went across the path and into the jungle but the twins had wisely stayed well hidden in the branches and leaves of the trees so the flying stink bomb missed them.

Psycho and the gang weren't so lucky. As intended, they got the full force of the shit. They were completely covered in black, stinking shit. It got into their eyes, their ears, their noses - and their mouths. They even swallowed some of it. A number of them were very sick in the next few days.

LITTLE DRAGON

A split second later, it got worse: the force of the blast blew them backwards. They staggered back... only to find air where their feet were expecting to find earth. Every one of them fell straight into the shit trench. It was just deep and full enough for them to be completely submerged for a moment. Those with their mouths open had the delight of having the shit from the heap which had got into their mouths washed down their throats into their stomachs. Having had the air knocked from their lungs by the force of the blast, they were just ready to take in a breath as their heads sank under the surface of the liquid shit.

Some landed on Old Phuoc's house as well. Not that it was easy to tell; the house had been so filthy beforehand.

Hung decided that he should keep out of sight. If Psycho saw him, then he would be dead. The same would go for the twins. It was hard though, to keep out of sight, because once Hung had got over the shock of the force of the explosion - and the complete success of his plan - he was rolling around on the ground, laughing his head off. Distantly, he could hear similar sounds coming from the twins who had come out of the edge of the jungle and were standing at the entrance to Old Phuoc's place, holding each other up as they split their sides laughing.

They were aware that they had to get away - and fast. Trying, unsuccessfully, to control their laughter, they dashed happily across the backyard of Old Phuoc's place, through the broken down rear fence and along the side of the rice field immediately behind, heading back towards the village.

It was tempting to come back down the path again with the rest of the villagers, who were starting to rush along the path to find out the cause of the explosion. They could try to hide in the crowd, but they knew that if Psycho or any of his gang saw any of them, they would be dead meat.

They therefore returned to the marketplace and made themselves as visible as possible to other people by being a thorough nuisance to those stallholders who hadn't hurried along the path to Old Phuoc's place. An added bonus: a lot of stalls had been left unattended by those going to the source of the explosion: the three kids helped themselves to a lot of "good stuff" that day!

While a few folks, Old Phuoc and his wife, in particular, were furious by what they found when they reached the end of the path, the vast majority of people thought what had happened to Psycho and his cronies was both richly deserved and hilarious. Psycho and the gang were the talk of the district - the province - for weeks afterwards. They tried to bluster it out but that seemed to make things worse. Psycho knew that Hung and the twins were responsible but he couldn't prove it, particularly when Hung had seemingly been absent from Old Phuoc's place and none of them had been seen there at all. Psycho was intensely disliked by lots of people and the general feeling was that he had got what he deserved. "Just what he needed" was a comment that was often repeated and agreed with.

All of the gang, particularly Psycho, had to put up with weeks of never-ending teasing: people walking past him holding their noses and making grunting noises like pigs or clucking like chickens and even some throwing buckets of water over him. Because everyone seemed to be looking out for him and his gang, so that they could take the piss out of him, Psycho found that there was no chance for him to hunt down Hung and take his revenge. He was being watched too much to give him the freedom to do that.

LITTLE DRAGON

So Psycho left the district. With that, his gang collapsed: he was what had held it together and with his departure, the gang was like a ship without a rudder. It soon crashed onto the rocks and broke up.

Hung was over the moon... But not for long.

CHAPTER SEVEN

A few days later, Hung was walking up the hill to his village when he heard it. The sound was like God was striking the ground. He felt a rumble under his feet and then a cloud of dirt and dust came towards him from the edge of the village.

"OH SHIT!" was the only thing that came to Hung's mind. He dropped the sack he was carrying and ran at top speed towards the cloud and the source of the noise.

His quadriceps were burning from the effort he put into running. As he approached the site, he saw a crowd of people rushing towards the blackened center of impact.

Hung's heart raced. It felt as if it was going to burst out of his chest. He had an idea - a horrifying idea - as to what had caused the explosion. In his mind, he recalled the havoc that a smaller but similar explosion had recently caused while they had been fishing - and, of course, the successful sting on Psycho. This one looked to be a disaster.

A multitude of possible causes for the explosion raced through his mind at once. His stomach cramped tighter and tighter. Panic started to grip him: his demons were telling him what had happened - and why - and it wasn't good for Hung.

LITTLE DRAGON

Once he was near the site of the explosion, he started to notice pieces of metal from shacks scattered about, along with more and more people rushing to the scene.

Hung had a difficult time getting closer because of the people scrambling and pushing frantically towards the source of the explosion - as well as others, in a panic, trying just as hard to run away... to anywhere... away from whatever had happened. Most people didn't know what had caused the explosion but the sight of the damage and the flying metal when the explosion happened was enough for them: they weren't going to hang around to find out.

Hung struggled through the crowd. He was continually being pushed all over the place. He almost fell over a number of times, but then did so. His foot tripped on something. He fell, face first, to the ground and spat out a mouthful of dirt. He looked back, towards his feet, to see what he had tripped him up.

There, on the ground, lay an arm with no body attached to it and with two of the fingers missing. The other fingers and the skin of the arm were scorched and hanging off it like tissue paper. Between the two remaining fingers was a thin cigarette, still glowing in the breeze. Hung's stomach immediately emptied its contents all over the ground. He knew that this was his doing. He picked himself up and continued, towards the mass of people.

He peered ahead of him: a small crowd huddled over someone, all trying frantically to help whoever it was. Pushing his way through the throng of people, he looked down to see Butch, the large boy that he had met last night, lying on the ground. He appeared to be breathing - just - but otherwise was not responding to either the voices of those who were trying to talk to him, or to those who were trying to lift him. Most of the skin on his face was charred like burnt meat.

His hair and the skin on one side of his head were burnt away, down to his skull. His shirt was tattered and had melted: it was sticking, like glue, to his burnt chest. Hung could see some of Butch's rib bones. His right arm was mostly gone and what was left was a useless stump: hanging meat was all that remained. The left arm was missing entirely. Villagers made an effort to wrap up and apply tourniquets to the stumps of his arms, trying in vain to stem the flow of blood. Not that it would do him any good now.

Hung turned on his heel and ran home at once, as fast as he could. He checked the secret stash under his sleeping pad: there he had hidden one of the packs that he had taken from the factory. It was gone! Shit! Shit! FUCK!! Now he knew that he was in deep trouble. Butch must have found out where he lived and nicked the pack for himself. Had he taken the other one?

Hung rushed outside and ran down the track a short way. There was a large heap of stones and rocks which someone, years ago, had left there in the hope that one day a particularly muddy section of the road would be filled in with the rubble. It had never happened and probably never would now. Just once in a while, Hung used the heap as a back-up stash. Thank fuck he had done so this time with the second pack... At least he hoped that he had been lucky.

Checking quickly that no one was watching, he scrabbled in the heap, heaving aside several heavy rocks. Phew!" The second pack was there - and from the briefest of glances inside the pack, Hung could see that the same number of detonators remained. As he started to replace the rocks on top of the remaining pack, he thought to himself: "From the size of the explosion that blew up Butch, he must have set all the detonators off at once. Are there any more out there?" However, he was not planning on bringing any more attention upon himself in order to find out if this was right. If he started sniffing around, others wouldn't take long to work out that he had been involved.

The thought struck him: *"How many others could have been hurt because he'd brought the stuff back to the village?"*

"Fuckin' Butch! So careless. He was there when Xiang told them of the risks. He was there when the detonator - with only a tiny piece of the explosives attached to it - had been set off. Yet still he had been smoking while carrying the pack - with the fuses, the detonators - and the explosives. What was the asshole thinking?! He was to blame for this,"

Hung tried telling himself this, but still the sinking dread of the consequences that his actions would bring down upon him gnawed at his mind, making it worse and worse the more he thought about it. From the size of the explosion and the devastation it had caused, not only to Butch but to the nearby buildings, all the explosives and the rest of the detonators left in the pack from under Hung's sleeping pad must have gone up at once, in one go.

Quickly, he finished piling the rocks back on top of the pack and hurried home, tiptoeing back into his room. He lay down on his sleeping pad. As he did so, his mother came through the door. Without warning, she grabbed Hung's arm, pulled him to his feet and threw him up against the wall.

"That boy is dead because of you!" she yelled. She didn't need any proof that Hung was involved - and responsible;

she just knew it. Not another word passed her lips as she picked up a thin bamboo cane, dragged Hung outside the house to avoid waking Quân and commenced to beat Hung - for the next thirty minutes.

Eventually, with sweat pouring from her forehead, Hung's mother became exhausted from her efforts of beating her son and finally decided to throw the cane aside. Everything had just become too much for his mother. She felt overwhelmed. She headed for the kitchen, sat down and cried herself to sleep.

While his mother slept, Hung packed up what little money and belongings he had into his small bag and, being careful not to wake Quân, headed out through his secret back door from the shack. He knew the village would not forget this. In the morning, when everything had calmed down a bit and people were getting over the shock of what they had seen, they would come looking for him.

He kept hearing his mother's words echoing back and forward in his head:

"That boy is dead because of you!"

The words were ringing in his ears, again and again. He hoped that if he went away, his mother would be spared from any backlash from the villagers because of his actions. Fat chance. However, that was all he could think to do. He figured that he had put his mother through more than enough. How many more "big" mistakes would he make before she finally snapped and killed him?

As he left the shack, he went immediately to the heap of rocks and stones again and quickly retrieved the second pack of detonators, fuses and explosives. It was the only thing he had which might be of any possible value - and that value was open to question anyway.

    He headed for the harbor. When he got there, he snuck into what appeared to be an empty hut near the pier. It was dark as pitch inside so he couldn't be sure what, if anything, the hut contained, but he was too tired to care. He curled up in his customary fetal position, squeezed ever tighter by the grip of the demons in his stomach. He felt that he was being swallowed up by the darkness. He was alone.

CHAPTER EIGHT

The voice asked, softly: "Who is it, Dad?" Hung had been woken by the soft voice of a young boy. The boy giggled for a moment. Then there was silence for a few moments. He heard footsteps walking away into the distance.

"I don't know, son. It looks like a weird kind of fish," a man answered.

Hung's head and body hurt so bad. He started to open his eyes but the sun's rays stung the pupils, making him stop that in a hurry. He saw just enough to realize that he was in a hut or shack. He shut his eyes again tightly - he just listened. He could hear someone moving around outside but no one came to him. He heard a sizzling sound: then the smell of cooking fish filled the air around him. Hung forced his eyes to focus, despite the dazzlingly bright sunlight which hit him full in the face, shining through the open door of the hut.

A short distance away, a man stood near a bamboo counter, cooking fish in a beaten-up metal pan on a roughly-made indoor fire pit. Hung's stomach rumbled so loud it sounded like his inner demons were coming to life. He put his hands over his stomach, trying to prevent the demons from making such a noise, but he was just too hungry. He was confused: why was he so hungry? He noticed that when he moved, his whole body would shake. He felt so weak. He noticed also that the wounds from his mother's beating were starting to form scabs over them.

"A stomach making sounds like that needs to be fed, I would imagine," said a firm but kind voice.

A tall man stood in front of him. Hung couldn't see him clearly as the man had moved so that his back was to the door: he stood between Hung and the sun as it shone into the shack. His face was in shadow.

Hung had no idea what to do. He jumped up and, as he was used to doing at home, started to straighten up the bags on the floor where he had been lying. He noticed fish parts on the floor. The tall man moved back to the fire pit and continued cooking the fish and prepping more. Hung grabbed what appeared to be basket meant for trash. He began collecting the fish parts that were lying around and putting them in the basket.

The man remained silent, still frying his fish. It seemed he was cooking up that old favorite: "Fish and *Khoai Lang*" - sweet potatoes. Hung kept his head low while continuing to collect the rubbish off the floor.

Once he had finished the preparation for their meal, the man stacked together four plates and headed outside to a small bamboo table, followed by a little girl who Hung had only just noticed: she had been hiding behind the counter, unseen in the darkness of the hut. She was about a year or two younger than Hung, he reckoned. The man stopped short of the doorway.

"Get another stool," he told the girl. She picked up a stool from near the door and carried it outside. The tall man followed behind her but stopped again in the doorway.

Hung scurried into a dark corner, waiting to see what would happen next. Leaving the doorway, the man briefly stepped out of sight before returning almost straight away. The little girl also came back in again briefly, then went out, this time carrying out a bamboo chair which she pushed up to the table while the man set out the plates.

Once the table was set, the man sat down with a young boy who was just a bit older than Hung. Hung thought to himself: *"These, I assume, are his daughter and son."* They each sat quietly as if they were waiting on something.

Then it happened: the event that would change Hung's life forever...

"Come and sit, Little Fish. We'll speak later," the man said to Hung in a voice with just a hint of sternness in its tone. There was also a strange kindness about the man that Hung sensed as he walked towards the table. The man waved his hand in Hung's direction, calling Hung forward, at the same time as he started to eat.

Hung was starving. He crept forward and slid onto the empty stool next to the table. He started to eat.

The man was skinny but nothing gave any sign of weakness in his body. He had an inner strength - or so it seemed to Hung. His hair was medium length and tied in a tail to the back of his head. He stood very straight, making him seem taller than he was, even though he wasn't strongly built. His hands were worn and heavily marked from old injuries, with many noticeable scars crisscrossing over them. His arms were covered in intricate and complicated tattoos. Hung could see from the man's eyes that there were untold stories of past hardships, deep within him - deep inside his mind. But somehow, the man seemed to be able to carry the weight of the world on his shoulders with ease.

Clearly, the two children were his. The likeness of them to the man was unmistakable. They seemed to have manners - something Hung had never seen in people before. If Hung was honest with himself, the man and his children all left him feeling a bit nervous.

The shack they were outside was small, but well built and would probably stand up to the worst of weather conditions - wind, rain... whatever Nature threw at it Everything inside was very basic and simple, but usable. Everything seemed to have a purpose and there was nothing extra or unneeded. No luxuries. The hut and its contents were clean and tidy: having very little meant that what the man had he seemed to keep in working order and in good condition.

After Hung finished eating, he noticed that no one left the dinner table, even though they were done. He waited: he saw that every move he made was being watched. Hung had been the last one to finish: the man seemed to be testing him.

"You're excused," the man said with a nod to the boy and the girl, who picked up their dirty dishes and headed into the hut. Hung rose to follow them, but the man raised his hand from the table. "Not you, Little Fish," he said in a calm voice.

Hung wanted to dash inside, back into the shadows, but he knew that in his condition it would be impossible to get far, so he sat back down.

LITTLE DRAGON

"Where are you from, Little Fish?" the man asked. Hung looked down at his lap, saying nothing.

"Hmm.. I see," the man said, shaking his head gently. "Let's start off with something simpler. A name perhaps... That is unless you want me to continue calling you Little Fish."

"My name... My name is... Hung," he answered in a quiet, nervous voice. Hung cleared his throat and tried again, this time with more confidence. "My name is Hung."

"Hello, Hung. My name is Chien. This is my store - and my home. The boy and girl are my children - Kim and Sen. You've been sleeping here for a few days while your injuries have been healing. I've fed you so I imagine you're no longer feeling so weak."

He was right; Hung's muscles were no longer shaking and the dryness in his throat was gone.

Chien took Hung outside and pointed at the worn and dusty dirt road outside the shop. "Down that road about a mile away is a well. There are two buckets near the store over there." Chien pointed towards two empty black five-gallon buckets.

"Come back with water from the well. When you return, come in through the back door. There'll be a hammock waiting for you." Chien headed back into the store.

No surprise: Hung was feeling a little lost and really didn't know what to do, so he just sat there for a while.

Time passed. Hung noticed that Chien and the kids remained inside the hut. Hung stayed where he was, thinking.

LITTLE DRAGON

He didn't know what to do. He thought about returning home to face the villagers - and to face his mother! What would the rest of the villagers do to him if he returned there? So Hung decided to go to the well.

"I guess that settles it then," he said to himself.

Hung gathered his strength, fighting against his muscles which were crying out for him not to move. His bones popped and creaked as he headed over to the side of the shop. He stumbled up to the wall, grabbed the two buckets and headed down the road.

"Daddy, do you think he'll come back?" Sen asked her father, looking out of the small window. She watched Hung walk slowly down the road.

"I don't know, Sen. His will is strong and he's focused, but he is not centered. And that can be a dangerous thing in anyone."

Chien grabbed a broom and started sweeping the floor.

"His character is kind, but he's poisoned by fear and loneliness. Without help, he'll soon be lost to those two evils for the rest of his life."

Kim gazed out of the window from behind Sen. "I hope he makes it," he said.

"Me too, son," Chien agreed, nodding his head. "Me too."

LITTLE DRAGON

Hung felt he had been walking for hours and wanted to stop to sit down for a bit, but he knew that if he did, it would probably mean not being able to get up again. His body was running out of the energy given to it by his last meal. He began regretting that he had concentrated so much on only filling his stomach with food and that he had not drunk anything while eating his dinner. Now he was feeling very thirsty and dehydrated. He noticed that he had stopped sweating a while back. That couldn't be good. The empty buckets were starting to feel heavier now. Hung had no clue what his plan would be for getting two full buckets back to the hut.

It was growing dark. He looked down the road. The well was still so friggin' far away! He thought about dumping the buckets and taking off. He dropped the buckets at his feet and looked down at them. He was fed up and getting a bit angry - with Chien and with himself. He looked up into the sky. The stars were coming out... A cool breeze blew over him, giving Hung the pleasure of its softness. He helped to calm him. He stood there, enjoying the breeze for a moment, looking down the road...

That was until a wind devil blew dirt and dust into his eyes. Hung's temper flared up. Out of frustration and annoyance, he lashed out with a swift, hard kick at one of the buckets. Yes, that sent the bucket flying - but he had nothing on his feet and he also stubbed his big toe - hard.

"Shit!! FUCK!!" Hung screamed, grabbing the remaining bucket before hobbling over to pick up the one he had just kicked.

"Now I gotta hobble back with my fuckin' broken toe and two fuckin' heavy buckets! GIVE ME A BREAK," Hung yelled, snatching at the first bucket. Angrily, he rubbed his feet back and forward in the dirt before beginning to limp down the road like a half-dead donkey.

A short distance down the road, Hung could see a badly built wooden well with what appeared to be a bucket tied to a rope lying next to it. He noticed that roads from other directions met up at this point, alongside the well.

A small smile crossed his face for a moment when he stopped. Pride filled his heart. He'd made it!

It was at that moment that he decided he would never quit on anything in his life.

Hung walked up and looked down into the well. He was surprised at how full it was. He lowered the bucket to fill it. After pulling up his first bucket of water, it was as if he had gone mad - he tipped water all over himself. It poured over his face and down his chest and back. He swallowed it as fast as he could, drowning his mouth until he heaved up, puking water back up through his mouth and nose.

Eventually, he slowed his gulping to large sips until his stomach was maxed out. Then he took a few brief moments of rest against the wall of the well... For an instant, he felt content. He could feel strength slowly returning to his body as the water entered his system, bringing life to his muscles. He looked up at the moon and stars which seemed to be staring back at him saying:

"GET BACK TO IT!!"

Hung sent a thought back to them: *"As you wish. So be it. Let's get this done!"*

LITTLE DRAGON

After taking a deep breath from the semi-cool air, Hung began filling the buckets again. He knew that his arms wouldn't be able to carry the two heavy buckets all the way back, so he looked around in the dark for something large and strong, like a branch.

Hung snapped a branch from a nearby tree. After breaking off the thinner parts and the twigs, he threaded the branch through the handles of the buckets then stepped in between them. He heaved the branch onto his shoulders, as if he was a small water buffalo. Then, once the buckets were balanced properly on his shoulders, he started back towards Chien's shop.

Chien watched the path carefully. His eyes were fixed, staring straight ahead, trying to pierce the darkness, straining to catch sight of Hung returning. It was difficult to put his finger on why he should feel it, but he felt drawn to the boy. Hung's character seemed genuine and keen. Chien wanted to share his knowledge with the boy to help him become strong, as he did with his own children.

"Aahh, you silly old man. Why do you always insist on taking in waifs and strays?" He scolded himself out loud, muttering in a whisper, while being careful enough not to wake his children.

Chien looked back along the short passage in this shack to where his kids were sleeping; then he gazed back out of the window. The night was playing tricks on his eyes as shadowy figures seemed to be lurking out there. Then, at last, Chien saw Hung appear slowly out from the darkness and into a patch of moonlight. A smile crossed Chien's lips once he noticed Hung's shoulder bar, carrying the two buckets of water.

LITTLE DRAGON

"Very good. Very clever, Hung," Chien whispered under his breath.

Chien grabbed some bread and a mug of clean water, setting them out on a plate next to the hammock he had waiting for Hung. Then he climbed into his own hammock and closed his eyes.

Hung opened the unlocked back door and entered as quietly as he could. His muscles were aching from the workload. The pain was terrible from all the bruises on both sides of his shoulders, just behind his neck - which the branch and the heavy load of water had given him. He noticed the few pieces of bread next to his hammock on the floor and quickly ate. Having a flashback of the nasty experience of vomiting water earlier, he decided to drink slower this time.

He had finished his task for the day. Having refueled his body, Hung walked into the store area and placed his plate and mug where he had seen the family putting other dirty dishes. Hung gave a sigh of relief then returned to the hammock and fell down into it, almost flipping it over. After regaining his balance, Hung fell asleep almost instantly. From deep within the shadows of another part of the shack, Chien smiled while watching Hung sleep.

The next morning, Hung woke up to the sound of more giggling and people moving around. There were voices in the background, speaking so softly that he couldn't hear what was being said. He could feel the heat of the day building up, making beads of sweat run down his face. He sat up, rubbing the sleep from his eyes.

His muscles were sore. They complained to him as he stood up from the hammock. His legs wobbled. He swayed while trying to catch his balance. He gave his muscles a quick stretch by reaching towards the ceiling and spreading his arms as far apart as he could. This caused his muscles to spasm and stop working completely. He fell to the floor like a rag doll. Just when Hung thought things couldn't get any worse, his calves and shoulders started to cramp up, causing him severe pain. He whimpered and then, wincing at the pain, started rubbing his calf muscles, hoping the cramp would release its grip - but it refused.

"You've put your body through a great deal and it may take a few days for your muscles to come to terms with what has happened to you. The cramps are because you haven't been drinking enough water." Chien handed him a cup of fresh cool water.

"Drink this and in a few minutes you'll feel better, Little Fish."

Hung snatched the drink, gulping it down immediately.

"If a person offers you something you should be considerate in return," Chien said, looking deep into Hung's eyes.

Hung bowed his head and offered the cup back. "Thank you, sir," he replied. He had been corrected and he felt ashamed.

"You've shown us your value here, Hung. You've worked and done so without question and that's valuable to me."

"Thank you, sir."

"There's breakfast for you," Chien replied as he pointed to the table. "Build up your energy again and we'll speak more when you're finished."

"Yes sir," Hung responded before rushing over to the table to eat.

Moments later, Chien came to the table and sat quietly next to him. He crossed his legs, resting his hands on his thighs while waiting patiently for Hung to finish his meal.

Hung tried not to notice Chien waiting for him, but it was difficult because of how strong Chien's presence felt to him. He would have found this unbearable - upsetting - from other people, but with Chien it was different. Chien always had a serious look on his face which seemed to be demanding instant obedience to his commands, but there was also a calmness to him. It was that way with almost everything he did. It felt like he was always testing or searching for something. For some reason, Hung liked it - kind of.

Once Hung had finished, Chien signaled for Sen to take Hung's plate for washing.

As Sen came up to the table, their eyes made contact. Her blushing smile gave her away even though she tried to rush away with his plate.

"Where do you live, Hung?" Chien asked in a soft voice.

Hung looked down at the ground, sighing, not wanting to answer the question.

"It is disrespectful not to look at a person speaking to you. We must always remember our manners. Doing so keeps us from becoming animals. 'Manners make the man'."

Hung looked up at Chien: "I have no home, sir."

"Very well," Chien replied. "How old are you?" Hung began lowering his eyes, ready to gaze down at the ground again, until he remembered the rudeness it implied.

"I don't know, sir. I don't remember. It was never important."

"That will not do," Chien replied sternly. "It'll be very difficult in life to succeed in the future if you do not at least know when you were born."

He looked more closely at Hung, looking closely at his face and body. He seemed for a moment or two to be mentally processing a great deal of information.

"Hmm... Taking in your height and build, I guess you're around my son's age which is nine years old." Chien smiled. "That would put you being born in around 1971 or 1972."

Chien stood and stepped into his shop. After rummaging about for a bit, he finally came out again holding a tray in his hands upon which were two small needles. He set the tray on the table and began tying the needles together with fine thread.

"Pass me that small bottle with the black liquid inside," he told Hung, pointing to a shelf behind him. Hung's face screwed up in disgust as he passed the bottle to Chien. He didn't like the look of what was inside it.

Chien rolled up his sleeves slowly and neatly, making sure they were level with each other. The more of his arms that were uncovered, the more tattooed markings were shown. It was like someone had been writing a story all the way up Chien's arms.

LITTLE DRAGON

Chien could see Hung gazing at all the tattoos he had collected over the years, each one telling the story of some event that Chien had been through in life. Some of the tattoos reminded Hung of the heavens and hells he had endured. Hell was better off forgotten but Heaven he wished he had never left - or to be more truthful - Heaven was what he wanted for himself.

"These marks are made to remind me of things better not forgotten. Certain times in my life and some of the philosophies I have come to understand I have put into writing on my skin," he explained.

"Just off the side of the road you went down earlier is a small pond. Go down there and clean up your body as best you can. Here is a rag you can use. And a new set of clothes for changing into."

Hung ran down the path again as instructed and, just as Chien had said, a little bit off the path was a pond. Walking down to the edge of the water, he noticed a rope strung between two small trees that was obviously put there to hang clothes for drying.

There was another boy on the other side of the pond, cleaning himself off as well, so he figured this must be the place. Hung dropped his rag and splashed into the water. The water seemed to sting and burn his scratches and wounds. Hung paused for a second, allowing the water to wash over them. He threw back his hands as if he had just thrown the weight of the world off his shoulders.

He fell backwards, sinking beneath the surface of the pond. He watched the covering of leaves on the trees above him from under the water. Above the leaves, the blue sky waved and swayed in the ripples that he was making from his splashing in the water. It was beautiful.

Coming up for air, Hung wiped the water from his face. He grabbed the rag from the ground and began to scrub the dirt from his body. The clear water quickly turned dark as it mixed with the dirt and mud with which he had been covered..

He thought about the tray that Chien brought out from the shop and all the tattooed drawings and writing that covered his arms. The contents of the tray made him nervous. He wanted to ask Chien all sorts of questions, but something inside him told him not to.

Hung didn't want to keep Chien waiting, so he scrubbed himself as quickly as possible and dried himself off. He threw on the clothes that were provided to him. Chien had let him sleep in late, so the day was nearing its end already. Hung realized that he must have been exhausted.

Once he made it back to the opening at the end of the path, he saw Chien still sitting at the table with the tray in front of him.

"So there was a boy under all that clay after all, Little Fish," Chien said, checking carefully Hung's skills at cleaning himself.

Hung gave a quick grin. That was all he could manage while still staring at the tray. Chien pointed to the stool that Hung noticed was always being chosen for him to sit upon.

"Sit down. This is a significant point in your life, Hung, and I want you to remember this day always. I wish you to experience having a birthday and I am going to give you a date, here on your finger, as a reminder."

Chien smiled at Hung, preparing his needles next to the bottle of black ink.

"I will never lie to you, Hung. If you wish to stay, I can teach you a great many useful things and give you a roof over your head. I only ask that you pull your weight and work without question. Is this acceptable to you?" he asked.

Hung thought, but only for a second.

"Yes sir," he replied.

"Give me your left hand," Chien told him, holding his hand out towards Hung. Hung put his hand on the table. It was shaking a little.

Chien reached down and picked up the needles that he had previously tied together, before dipping them into the ink. He paused for a moment, then looked into Hung's eyes.

"This is going to hurt. Bite on this if you need to." Chien handed him a short stick.

For the next thirty minutes, while the sun began to set, Chien repeatedly jabbed the needle into Hung's skin at the base of one of his fingers - one finger after another. Blood trickled out from the pores.

From time to time, Chien took a clean cloth and wiped the blood away before continuing. Hung refused to let himself cry out in pain: he sat there silently as streams of tears ran down his cheeks. Then it was over.

"Now... you are no longer a Little Fish, are you?" Chien said to him, at the same time bandaging Hung's fingers. "You are more like a Dogfish now - a little Shark. Now go and clean up."

Over the next few weeks, Chien asked Hung many questions about his past and how he had survived. With each story told - particular moments that Hung recalled - Chien would pick a spot on Hung's body and ink, in Sumi ,characters describing what was to be remembered.

After the fingers on his left hand had received the tattoo treatment, next came his right forearm. The inking recorded his life on the street, dealing with bullying and how Hung despised being poor. Also, the times he had been kicked, beaten or separated from his friends and loved ones. Then his chest became the next canvas for the history of Hung.

After an inking session which lasted a really tough couple of hours, Hung picked his head up off the table and saw the phrase *"Kiếp Nghèo Ôm Hận"* had been inked on his forearm.

"Poor fortune breeds hatred," Chien explained to him. "When a person is beaten a lot then there comes a point - a point of no return - when their heart can become darkened, angry, hardened. The only feeling they have left is hate."

Chien tried to cheer up Hung, seeing the worried look in his eyes: "I will show you other ways; an alternative way to live your life."

After Hung had told Chien all that he had to tell, Chien told him to remove his shirt. Almost two hours later the words ***"Bụi Đời"*** were inked across his chest.

"This is to remind you always where you came from. It means **"Child of the Streets"**. The things that I will teach you will test you. You will learn things from both sides of the line. The inner strength that you have now must remain with you and shine bright always. You have more qualities within you than you know. I can see that. If the brightness ... the quality ... of your strength starts to darken or fade, you may fail yourself and others. If it darkens too much, you will become lost."

From that moment on, Hung's life and how he lived it was tied firmly to Chien and how Chien lived his life. Chien knew that Hung had to be kept occupied; his brain was too active to be left without something to divert his attention. Hung was put to work in the marketplace shop, dealing with the customers and also learning how to butcher meat.

Chien taught him how to kill pigs and chickens, ready for sale: hanging them upside down by their legs, making sure that there was a bowl underneath them to catch the blood, then slitting their throats quickly and cleanly with the sharpest knife they had, so as to cause as little suffering as possible. Hung quickly became skilled with the knife - how to handle it and what could be done with it. Any knife in his hand soon felt as if it was an extension of his arm.

Having finished off a pig, Hung was shown how to cut it up into joints, ready to go on the meat counter. Chickens would sometimes be sold in pairs: sometimes plucked and drawn; other times still with their feathers and innards in place. Increasingly Hung became a very useful and experienced pair of hands around the shop. And trustworthy too, which was of great comfort to Chien.

Chien began to be more than just a teacher. More than just a mentor. Hung knew things would not be easy; all he would learn would come at a price, but it was a price he was willing to pay. He felt strangely excited to find what the days ahead would bring.

He wondered what the future held in store for him.

CHAPTER NINE

The next morning, Hung woke up with a new-found energy, immensely excited as to what the day would bring. He soon realized that the morning breakfast routines in Chien's house were like a ritual - a set pattern which kept everything to a strict schedule.

Everyone still ate at the table in almost complete silence and, when excused, each person would wash their dishes before sitting back down and awaiting Chien's instructions for the day ahead.

"We need to get the boat ready for another trip. It's time for us to go back out to sea," Chien began to explain. "We are short of both fish and crab and our other supplies are getting low," he continued.

Chien gestured to Kim. "I need you and Sen to chop up some sticks for the fire, ready for cooking, while Hung and I collect the fruit and vegetables from the shop. We'll start loading the boat once we have everything together."

Kim and Sen rushed off to do as they were instructed. They were very excited to be leaving on the boat again. Hung stood there, waiting for Chien to give him more instructions about his tasks. Chien signaled Hung to follow him.

LITTLE DRAGON

"Since I have asked so much of you, I felt that telling you a bit more about me would only be fair." He glanced at Hung as they walked slowly towards the shop. "What seems like a lifetime ago, my life was very different from the one you see now. I've seen many places and met many different people," he told Hung as they entered the shop.

Chien picked up some wooden crates to use for carrying stores down to the boat. Listening intently to Chien's story, Hung helped pack crate after crate with supplies. Chien went on to tell Hung stories of the great bravery and determination shown by the people during the war between the Americans and the Vietnamese.

Chien continued, explaining to Hung: "A long time ago, I lived in South Vietnam and I would take my boat - the boat you are about to see - up the coast to North Vietnam, bringing back supplies and weapons to soldiers fighting the Americans in the south. To do this, I had to be a smuggler."

Hung's eyes lit up with fascination as he continued helping Chien with the packing of the containers. He was excited about going to the boat. He had never been on anything other than a small rowing boat before. He was quickly hooked by the story that Chien was telling. "I infiltrated American strongholds to steal information," Chien continued. "I would then take this information back to the Resistance. These were the most common missions."

During the telling of his tale, Hung could see and hear the pride build up inside Chien as he spoke of his country and the people he was fighting to protect. Hung could tell that Chien's homeland and his family were his heart and soul. Chien found that he enjoyed talking to Hung; he found him to be a good listener. Chien relaxed more and more as he went on.

The stories that were the most interesting were the ones of Chien's secret, undercover, missions. Keeping to the shadows to penetrate deep into the enemy-held territory, slipping in and out like a ninja. Sailing repeatedly up and down the coast, always on the lookout for the authorities and hoping to avoid the naval patrol ships. Hung now realized that the boat meant a huge amount to Chien: it has been the place where he felt the safest. It was almost like another child to him.

They walked down to the harbor together and Hung saw Chien's boat for the first time. He was used to seeing boats, of course - he would watch them from the shore, both out at sea and also on the river, but this one seemed so much bigger close up.

Chien had been calling it a boat - but it was in fact a traditional Vietnamese junk - locally built and high at both ends - stem and stern. This one was a bit larger than most of the others in the harbor and even to Hung's inexperienced eyes, he could see that it was built stronger, with thicker timbers, than the others nearby. It stood out.

Then he remembered: Chien had already told Hung that boats were female and referred to as "she". Hung could see that "she" was called High Tides.

Over the next few days, Chien would carry out maintenance to High Tides, cleaning and patching her with the deep care of a man who wouldn't want to live without her. Chien could see Hung looking at the junk and that he was developing an interest in her.

LITTLE DRAGON

Chien's mind drifted back to the time when he had sailed away from the war - the day it was finally over. The first thing he did after the war was travel to Hanoi, then finally to Hon Gai, doing again what he knew best; sailing. As it would turn out, mentoring and guiding lost children was what had transformed him into the man he was now.

Hung looked up at Chien with a confused look on his face. "I have a question, sir," he said. Chien responded with a smile. "If you ask, I will do my best to answer. You may ask me anything; that is the way of things. People will always need other people to answer questions, otherwise we are fated to miss out in life."

Hung nodded his agreement, telling him: "As far back as I can remember, every time I disagreed with someone or got into trouble, I was beaten and told this is how you learn right from wrong. I've been here a long time and as many things as I have gotten wrong, you have only spoken to me about how to correct what I did wrong. How come you never hit me?" Hung asked with humility.

Chien thought carefully about how best to answer Hung's question for quite some time. He couldn't summon up the courage to ask why Hung had asked such a question. He couldn't recall a time when he had been so truly angry as to become violent. He was one of the calmest people you could ever meet.

"Ahhh," he said at last, with a start of a grin on his face. "An excellent question. I can see it took quite a bit of courage for you to ask it." Hung felt a little more at ease since Chien thought it was a good question.

Chien said: "I like to follow a set of philosophies - values and beliefs - that guide me through life and the many decisions it asks you to make. Each has its own standard to guide you. They set standards for you. Then you'll do the right thing. Do you understand?" he asked Hung.

"I think so," Hung replied, certain that he had at least got the hang of what he had been told.

Giving a small chuckle, Chien continued: "Let me try to explain what I mean. This is one of my favorite philosophies. It says: 'Teaching based on negative discipline builds obedience, but teaching based on trust and understanding builds loyalty'. Such teaching includes discipline when needed, but it is not negative discipline: it is positive."

Hung looked at Chien. He was disappointed with himself. "I don't think I quite understand, sir."

"Let me put it another way." Thinking for a moment, he rubbed the stubble on his chin a few times then continued. "I could hit and beat you until you got things right and I'm certain you would do so, but in your heart, you're fearing the pain." Chien once again gave a gentle smile.

"That method of forcing a student to be obedient gets what the teacher wants at the time, but anyone can come along and turn you against a violent teacher through a simple act of kindness. However, if your teacher shows you what you did wrong and lets you know that it is all right to make mistakes, then as long as you learn from those mistakes, it is more than likely that you'll come to love and be loyal to your teacher. The teacher still uses discipline by making sure that you concentrate, study hard and feel able to ask questions, but it is not a violent discipline. The bond between a good, kind, teacher and the student is much more difficult to break.

LITTLE DRAGON

Now do you understand?" he asked Hung.

"I do, sir. Thank you," Hung answered.

Early in the evening, once everything was prepared on board, Chien took High Tides out to sea a few miles from the coast to do some light fishing, mainly for fish for their daily meals. He went by himself. Chien never went any further than that without taking the children, just in case he had to hurry back should anything happen. If there was an emergency, the kids were instructed to light a signal fire on the seashore. Chien showed them that throwing onto the flames a particular white powder which he had given them caused a thick black smoke signal that could be seen for miles.

After a few hours, he returned to port. When Chien arrived, the children were waiting for him on the dockside. They helped him tie up High Tides alongside the quay where all the rich people docked their boats. Hung watched a number of dead bodies - refugees - being dragged away from in front of some of the ships in the harbor. Their crews would land the bodies on the quayside, from where they would be stacked up on a wagon, ready to be transported away for cremation. Away from the docks and the marketplace.

"I would like you to come with me tomorrow to the market, once we clean today's fish.

"Yes sir," Hung exclaimed, excited to be going to the market again. Even though Hung knew Chien wouldn't be talking to him much when he had business to do, Hung enjoyed going to the market with him; he liked its sights, smells and the general hubbub.

LITTLE DRAGON

In addition to the ordinary men and women who visited the market day by day, there were four other different kinds of people in the market.

The Merchants were the first. They were all the people, including Chien, who sold what they had at the marketplace. Chien worked out of a small hut where he cleaned and sold fish, along with crab, octopus - basically, anything that he caught.

Sweat ran down the sunburnt faces of the Merchants. They had the smell of hard work about them. Their hands were hardened and rough from the rigors of their daily routine.

The second kind of people were 'The Rich'. They came to buy supplies for their homes and their big estates. They came to the market mainly to buy cheap, lower quality food for their home and domestic staff, who were usually beaten and generally treated with contempt and often with much cruelty by their employers. Those kind of people were easy to spot - wearing their fine silks and with dirt-free faces. They walked around in their clean clothes, smelling of sweet lavender soap. Their soft skin appeared radically different from the weather-worn skin of the hard-working merchants and others around them.

Then there were the Gangsters - the ones that fed off everyone else, like sharks in a pool. Smelling blood and rushing in every time they sensed fresh meat. Always making sure that they kept control of their "patches"; a beating here, a stabbing there, a person strung up from the rafters in their shop. They were always leaving a reminder somewhere, to make sure everyone knew who was the boss. They were the difficult ones to spot; they knew how to blend in and to stay in the shadows. Often they just took money from the merchants' bags, right under their eyes, just to prove - to the other gangsters as well as the rest of the population - just who was really running things. That showed power!

Last, there were the Minorities - the sub-class of people. The people that everyone else didn't consider people. The ones you could kick around and walk on as you pass through. The ones that took your wallet when you knocked them down to the ground. The Chinese and Half-Breeds - including Hung - fell into this group.

But people liked Hung. Or at least he felt that they liked the new person he had become, thanks to Chien. A small sense of pride warmed Hung's insides. It felt as if that growing pride was putting his demons in a choke hold, throttling them, forcing them to submit.

In the short time that Hung had been staying with Chien and his family, he realized how much he had learned. Sen had started to spend a few hours each day with Hung, teaching him how to read and write in Vietnamese. She was a good and patient teacher. Chien had told him how important it was to understand his own language. Hung felt like a member of the family here, unlike with his parents, or in any other place he had been. Here he felt attached; he felt that he had a home, a place with roots. Chien always reminded his children and Hung of the importance of confidence and self-worth. The understanding of this kept their minds in a good place.

Having finished cleaning and packing up the fish the night before and after a few hours' sleep, they headed out for the marketplace at the crack of dawn. It wasn't far from the dock side and they arrived there during the early morning.

"Today, Hung, I will need you to help me with something important and very dangerous," Chien told him. Hung's eyes lit up. "I need you to trust me fully and do exactly what I say - nothing more. If you can do this for me, I will have something special for you in return. Does this interest you?" Chien asked.

"Yes, I'll do it, sir," Hung replied.

"Excellent," Chien exclaimed with a smile. "A very good friend of mine has had something taken from him. He would like me to get it back. In order for everything to work, I have to ask you to do something," he continued. Hung was curious and excited. However, he knew enough not to ask more. Never ask questions: it was something he had learned at home from his mother and father. "Don't ask, don't tell" was the strict rule that had been drummed into him from as early as he could remember.

Hung nodded. His voice wobbled a bit. "I will, sir."

"Excellent!" Chien repeated. He handed Hung a small flat bag. "Take this satchel and strap it under your shirt, around the waist. You'll be looking for a very small item, wrapped in a blue cloth. When you find it, put it in the satchel and buckle it in tight. Do not open up the cloth under any circumstances. What is inside it is none of your concern. Do you understand?"

LITTLE DRAGON

Hung could tell Chien was very serious about that part so he responded straight away: "Yes sir."

Chien continued to explain: "Now, here is the hard part, Hung. To make sure that the thief doesn't do this to anyone else, we want to get the police involved and for them to come to the thief's house."

Hung interrupted Chien: "This way he can't do it to anyone else? How come?"

Chien took a deep breath: this was the hardest part to explain - the part that he didn't want to have to ask Hung.

"The thief will want to take the thing back from you. He will be desperate to do so".

Chien sighed heavily and explained further: "In order for this to work we need you to let him catch you. Which means that, more than likely, he is going to beat you to a pulp before he can be stopped. When he starts doing so, the police will be called and they will come to assist. Understand?"

Hung frowned. "I don't like this plan much any more."

Chien placed his hand on Hung's shoulder. "Just remember: you're doing it for the greater good. Remember too that there's nothing to fear but your fear. I know it is a lot to ask of you, but if the police come, they will keep an eye on the man in the future. He won't be keen to explain to the police that you have taken something from him when he had stolen it in the first place - and he probably won't notice that you have taken it until after you are out of the house."

Chien had had his own kids steal things as a test of their

survival skills and for practice, but he had never asked any of them to get caught on purpose. Previously, it had always been a test of not getting caught or of how to stay hidden - things like that.

He felt bad about putting Hung in harm's way, deliberately. Hung was worried but he didn't want to disappoint Chien and he really didn't want to miss out on the sweet treats that Chien gave to those who completed tasks successfully. It is always a good day when you get the job done!

"I can do it, sir," Hung told Chien.

"What a brave soldier you are, Hung," Chien replied. "The house we are looking for is a couple of blocks away down this alleyway."

Chien and Hung started walking in the direction of the house. Shadows crept around them. Suddenly, Hung felt someone bump into him. Hung turned sharply. "Excuse me," said a young boy, just a little bigger than Hung. As the boy was speaking, Hung felt a sharp pull on the satchel strapped to his side.

The pickpocket obviously didn't expect it to be strapped so firmly to Hung. Hung widened his stance, which stopped the actions of the slightly larger boy, then Hung shoved him backwards. Once the boy was off balance, Hung spun around and punched the boy full square on the nose. The pickpocket stumbled, let go of the satchel and fell to the ground. He looked up at Hung as Chien was stepping in behind him.

"Wow!" the boy said, shaking the cobwebs from his clouded head. "You pack a pretty hard punch for a small guy!" he said, wiping the blood which by then was streaming from his nose.

Hung felt a rush of pride filling his chest as he gave a grin. Hung looked up at Chien. Chien gazed down at the boy on the ground, then reached out his hand to help him up.

"Hung's had a great deal of practice in this particular area," Chien explained. "What's your name, boy?" Chien asked as he helped him to his feet.

"Nhât," the boy answered.

Hung smiled inwardly: Nhât looked a lot like his old friend Tranh, back in the village. He even moved his body in ways similar to Tranh too, he thought.

"You gonna call the authorities on me?" Nhât questioned.

"Maybe," Chien said, frowning at Nhât.

"Or maybe he could help us, sir?" Hung suggested, looking at Chien.

"Indeed. Maybe he could, Hung. Clever thinking," Chien replied.

Chien agreed, knowing that this pickpocket would have no difficulty in accepting any better option for dealing with the situation he found himself in. After a brief explanation to Nhât from Chien, the three were off again to their destination.

"This man is wealthy and has a large house, so what does that tell us, Hung, about where to find what you are going to be looking for?" Chien asked.

Hung instinctively replied: "More than likely what I'm looking for will be in his bedroom chamber or his study room, sir."

"Good thinking, Hung. That's a great mind you have, son," Chien said with a grin. "Remember, Nhât: when I give you the signal, run for the authorities, as quick as you can." Nhât nodded and replied with a smirk, "I will." Like Hung had done, Nhât had worked out quickly that Chien was a good person to know.

With that, the two boys raced towards the side of the target building, next to a window. Nhât squatted down, bracing his hands on his knees as Hung climbed up his back and through the open window. Since Hung had practiced this routine so many times when escaping bullies and climbing over walls and fences, he was virtually silent when he landed, hitting the floor softly inside of the room. Once Hung was inside, Nhât ran around to the front door to keep watch, waiting for Chien's signal. Chien hid in the shadows at the corner of the building. When the signal was given, Nhât was to run off and bring the police.

Inside, Hung scanned the room to check if anyone was there, but the room was empty. It appeared to be a small, simple, kitchen with pots and pans and a sink. He could see through an open doorway to another room which contained a table and a few chairs. That looked like it could be the sitting room.

Hung crept over to the doorway and peered around the corner of the door, into the sitting room, but there was no one there either. He tiptoed across the room and then a bit further, along to the next room from where noises were coming and where he saw a big fat guy lying on a sweat-soaked bed, snoring and with his mouth hanging open. He looked like a pig - the Pigman.

Hung screwed up his face in disgust as he watched a line of drool slide down the side of the fat man's face into his greasy, matted and dirty hair on the pillow.

Hung saw the blue cloth that he was after lying on a chest next to the bed. His heart began racing as he crept closer and closer. The Pigman had the most foul breath - or it could have been his body odor: Hung couldn't quite tell. It made him feel like hurling: it was a struggle not to throw up there and then. Hung picked up the cloth, being careful not to drop it or its contents. He slid it inside his satchel closed the clasp tightly and did up the buckle.

Now for the hard part. His heart started beating double time. From a nearby cabinet, he picked up the most expensive-looking breakable thing he could see - a really big fine china bowl. Hung lifted the bowl high above his head and just let it drop. The crash was loud and could be heard from quite a distance away. Chien heard the crash and he signaled for Nhât to go fetch the police.

The Pigman tried to jump up from the bed. He was squealing like a pig being struck with a red hot poker. He fell out of bed onto the floor: THUMP!

The Pigman yelled as loud as he could. "THIEF!" He stumbled over towards Hung, trying to grab him.

Hung wanted to bolt straight out of the front door as fast as he could, but he knew he couldn't. He had to stay: that was part of the plan.

After a few seconds of stumbles and falling over his own feet, the Pigman finally got up. He wondered why Hung hadn't bolted out of the room. He grabbed Hung by the arm, raising his gigantic fist and smashing it into Hung's cheekbone. The hit created a sound like a firecracker going off. It seemed to reverberate through the room, bouncing off the walls.

Hung's vision exploded into a blinding flash of yellow light. The impact threw him to the floor. The Pigman noticed Hung trying to pick himself up and so he threw himself at Hung violently, kicking him several times in his ribs. A few of the kicks struck Hung in his upper leg area, stopping him from getting up. Other kicks landed on Hung's stomach so hard he almost vomited. The breath flew out of Hung's lungs. He was gasping for air as he tried repeatedly to get to his feet.

The Pigman grabbed a nearby walking stick and started beating Hung with it. Hung thought to himself: "What could be taking them so long?" He could feel lumps and bruises forming all over his back.

Immediately following the next whack on his back, Hung heard the front door bang open. A police officer rushed into the room. He was the first witness to the Pigman beating up a boy. Another few whacks landed on Hung's back before the Pigman recognized the officer. Instantly he stopped beating Hung and started running his mouth off, shouting at the officer with his version of everything that had just happened. He made a huge fuss about the broken bowl and how valuable it was. He didn't notice that the blue cloth and its contents had disappeared. Not that he would have said anything, even if he had done so.

Moments later, the officer picked Hung up from off the floor. "Why do street trash like you always cause trouble?" he grumbled, throwing Hung out of the front door of the house. The policeman assumed that Hung had been in the house either to steal small items of little value and had been caught before he could do so, or he was a vandal. He didn't think to search Hung and he didn't spot the satchel, which was still well hidden under Hung's shirt.

No one stopped to wonder why Hung hadn't fled when the Pigman had woken up... why Hung had seemingly stayed there, deliberately, so that he would be beaten up.

After Hung had been ejected, the police officer turned and started apologizing to the sweaty Pigman. That was the easiest thing to do, the policeman reckoned: he didn't like the Pigman and wanted to get away as quickly as he could. By the time that the Pigman woke up to the missing blue cloth, Hung was long gone.

CHAPTER TEN

Nhât rushed to Hung, helping him back over to Chien as quickly - and gently - as possible. Hung's whole body was screaming at him in agonizing pain. Chien carried Hung to the tiny hut which stood behind his stall, off to one side of the market. Nhât followed, a look of concern on his face. He had only met Hung for the first time a few minutes before, but even in that short time, he had come to realize just how brave Hung was - and what a terrible beating he had taken.

Chien lowered Hung slowly and carefully onto a cloth laid over the table inside the hut. The intense pain from the kicks to his stomach had Hung curling up, gripping his stomach.

Chien carefully cut away Hung's shirt, exposing the swollen lumps and bruises that had been caused by the beating with the stick. The lumps, bruises, swellings and grazes seemed to cover every part of him, making him look like some sort of alien creature. Some wounds were so bad that the skin had split open and were bleeding, while others were starting to turn black and blue.

Chien rummaged around in the back of the hut for a moment, then dragged a two-foot long chest out from one corner over to the table. From inside it, he took out two small containers - two bottles or vials each containing a liquid -

together with a small pouch and a mortar and pestle. Hung began groaning louder and louder. Chien reached over to his side, then poured some water out of a jug into a bowl, which he set beside Hung.

Chien opened one of the bottles and poured some of its contents into a cup.

"Drink this, Hung," he said, putting the cup into Hung's hands.

Hung tilted his head back, trying to take a sip. It made him start to cough. Chien took out dried plants from the pouch and put them into the mortar. He took another container from the chest and opened it. It contained a powder, a pinch of which Chien added to the dried plants. He started grinding the mixture in the mortar forcefully with the pestle.

Once he had achieved a fine powder, he added it to the water in the bowl beside Hung. He continued mixing it with a small bamboo spoon until it became a smooth creamy ointment. Chien spread the ointment across the open wounds. He used bandages to dress them and to try to keep them clean. He added more water to the rest of the ointment, making it more like a lotion which he proceeded to rub all over Hung's body. "This will soothe your muscles," he told Hung.

After examining the rest of Hung's body, Chien turned his attention to Hung's legs. Both were badly hurt but he noticed how severe the bruising and swelling was on Hung's right leg. From the darkness of the bruising, it was more than likely to be broken. Chien applied some of the lotion to it, then hurried out into the market where he managed to get hold of some ice. He crushed up the ice and wrapped it up in a cloth which he tied carefully and gently to Hung's leg.

Hung's eyes started to close. He'd lost all his energy. The pain from his wounds was taking over: his body was wanting to shut itself down to give it a chance to heal. Within a few more moments he was unconscious, with Chien still watching over him. Hung's muscles began to relax as the deep sleep of unconsciousness overtook him, thus making Chien's job much easier.

Chien finished doing what he could for Hung's wounds and particularly the injured leg. After he was finished, he gestured to Nhât to step outside the hut so that Hung's sleep would not be disturbed - not that a lumbering giant could wake him right now.

...Struggling on through the crowd, continually being pushed all over the place... his foot tripping on something. What was it? Falling to the ground... spitting out dirt. What had tripped him up??

An arm but no body. Fingers missing. Fingers and skin... burnt - peeled away and hanging off it. Throwing up... It was all his fault... Get up! Whose arm is it? Where is he?.

A body on the ground.

Who? Who is it? Help him!!

Butch! It's Butch. He's alive? Yes: he's alive! He's breathing - but...

LITTLE DRAGON

His face! His head! Burnt. Oh fu... fu... Fuck!

Oh shit!!... His body! His ribs are showing. What's happened to his arms??!

The bleeding!! Stop the bleeding. Someone stop the bleeding!

Butch!! Wake up!! Wake up!!...

Hung thrashed around violently as the nightmare seized him tighter and tighter. It was so vivid. Hung was back there, in the village. It was so real to him, but then, gradually, it became blurred in his mind as he struggled to open his eyes. The nightmarish scene started to fade as he crawled back to consciousness.

"Easy, Hung," a calm voice said to him soothingly.

Hung began to open his eyes, but the light really hurt them so he shut them before trying again to open them - this time more slowly - once the pain from the first attempt had reduced. He tried to move, but his muscles cried out for him to stay put. All he could manage after his efforts to sit up was a groan.

"You have been asleep for more than a day, Hung. Don't try to get up. Keep lying down. You must take things slowly. Your body has suffered a lot of damage and it needs time to heal."

That much Hung was sure of. No arguments from him on that score. Everything hurt!

Hung rolled onto his back but couldn't tell if that was better

LITTLE DRAGON

or worse. However, by doing so it meant that he was no longer facing the light from the open door which did reduce the pain in his eyes. His muscles felt weak and cramped up when he tried to move, so he stopped trying. Chien reached onto the table, picked up a long thin cylinder and looked down at Hung.

"Drink this." He put the cylinder to Hung's mouth, tipped it up and emptied the liquid contents into his mouth. It was just enough for a small drink.

Immediately Hung screwed up his face because of the extreme bitterness of the drink - all the more so since he had been expecting water.

"Oh yes," Chien chuckled, "I forgot to mention the bitterness!" Chien was almost laughing.

Hung wasn't laughing, although perhaps he might have tried if he knew that it wouldn't hurt him too much. He wasn't going to risk it - so he just grinned.

Before he drifted back to sleep again, he heard Chien say to him:

"Well done, Little Fish. You were very brave." Chien paused before continuing:

"You need a new name; you're not a little fish. Let's call you "Little Dragon"... Yes, that suits you... Little Dragon".

Hung's heart filled with joy and price. He loved the name. Fierce, strong, powerful - and fiery. Yes, that would suit him. He didn't think any more about it for the time being, as the call of sleep was overpowering.

LITTLE DRAGON

Hung opened his eyes slowly this time around. A good deal of the pain in his body seemed to be gone so he now could actually move a bit. *"How long have I been asleep this time?"* he asked himself.

Chien would be disappointed by his lack of effort. Rolling from his back to his side and after a struggle, Hung pushed himself slowly with both arms into a sitting position. Sitting upright, he let out a deep breath from the effort. His muscles quivered and cramped from the lack of proper food and nutrients that he should have been having. The healing that was going on in his body had used up what little reserves his body held.

Chien watched Hung's efforts. "Good, that medicine seems to be working," he said. "I don't have much left until I get more plants to make it with, so I will have to use the rest sparingly. It should last long enough." Chien gave him another dose of his potion, the mixture from the bottle, and then went outside.

Whatever it was, Hung liked it… well maybe not the taste.

How long was I asleep for this time?" Hung called out to Chien, speaking his thoughts.

"Just a little while this time," a familiar voice said.

Hung couldn't quite make out the voice so he looked over towards where the voice had come from. Nhât was at the counter, cleaning fish, packing some for selling and some for transport back to High Tides.

"Nhât?" Hung said in what was still a very dry and raspy voice.

"Oh, right. Here, have this," he said, bringing over a wooden cup with some semi-cool water in it. "Chien said to drink it slowly," Nhât instructed.

"I did indeed," Chien said, coming back inside again and moving quietly and stealthily up behind Nhât, making him jump.

"Damn! He's good," Nhât said in a whisper to Hung who had a smile on his face.

"You get used to it," Hung said, still grinning.

"I couldn't believe it when he asked me to stick around," Nhât said excitedly.

"I can," Hung replied, knowing it had happened several times before to others in addition to himself.

"Nhât will be joining us on our voyage this time since he has already proven his value," Chien said, with a nod of approval towards Nhât. "He's good at adapting to his surroundings like you are, Hung - and his intentions have been honest since trying to pick your pocket. I think his character and skills will fit in and be useful."

Chien looked over to Hung and saw the accepting, even happy, look on his face. "I can see you have no objections and since he is the largest of you children, his strength will be useful as well."

LITTLE DRAGON

Chien handed Hung a thick strip of meat. It had been cooked in something very sweet, perhaps honey. The meat had sucked up much of that sweetness. Hung took it from Chien and bowed his head in appreciation.

"Thank you, sir," he said, then gobbled it up with a smile.

The sweetness melted into his tongue as he chewed the meat and his body felt giddy from the sudden rush of sugars into his bloodstream. Hung swung his legs back and forth, enjoying every chew and swallow. Chien helped Hung stand up from the low cot. Putting pressure on his leg caused Hung to wince and immediately he started to favor it, putting more weight on the less injured leg - although that was sore too.

"Your leg: it's broken. Not badly, but it's going to hurt for a while. After a few days, it'll get much easier. For now, use this."

Chien handed Hung a thick, strong home-made crutch to help support his weight.

"Thank you, sir."

"There's a proper meal just outside on the table. Go and eat so your body may heal quicker. We'll head out a bit later," Chien instructed.

After Hung had finished eating the meal he was given, which was much larger than usual, he felt much better. He could feel energy returning to his body, although the bruising and sores were really beginning to hurt again. They were starting to throb. Nevertheless, he stood up and carried his dirty dishes over to Nhât who was doing the washing up.

LITTLE DRAGON

"Here, Hung, drink this," Chien instructed him, as he came up suddenly behind the boys. Again Nhât was startled and jumped whereas Hung did not.

"Oh no: not again!" Nhât exclaimed, startled again by Chien's silent approach. Hung took a small bottle from Chien, then drank the contents which again were the same bitter liquid. Even with such a small amount in the bottle, the bitterness was too sharp for Hung and again he made a face. Chien smiled, then picked up a large satchel from under the counter, slung it over his shoulder and herded the two boys out of the back door, where Kim and Sen were already waiting.

"Hi, Hung." Sen spoke up first.

"Hey guys," Hung responded.

We are going over to the east side of town today," Chien instructed them, leading the way. Hung did the best he could not to delay them: he was trying to get used to the crutch.

Before long they reached a rundown, abandoned, house on the edge of town, where the jungle pressed down to the built-up area, near to the harbor. The house had no door and smelt of bad fish and urine. No doubt it was a roof for homeless kids - an overnight shelter of sorts - as well as being used by the local thieves as a place to hang out during the hours of darkness.

"Today we play a special kind of game," Chien began. "I like to call this one "Tag the Man!" It teaches us stealth and how important it is to be aware of our surroundings. It'll help you when we go to the island to hunt and track game." Chien began explaining what they would be doing. He had their fullest attention. Mention of the island was exciting for the children, particularly Hung and Nhât.

Chien had a certain way with words and his voice which Hung could not quite explain. The way he spoke and his tone of voice simply made you want to listen to him - a true storyteller: a motivator.

From his satchel, Chien pulled out four thin metal tubes. They were about the size of small pencils and each had one end sharpened to a point. The children didn't know it, but the sharpened point was on a spring and it would be drawn back into the tube when pressed on that end. It was a form of syringe. Chien held the tubes out in front of him for each of the kids to inspect. He gave one to each of them in turn: Kim, Sen, Hung and Nhât.

"Don't touch the tips of your tube or you'll damage it. That's very important. It's vital too that you hold it along the sides when you use it. You must be careful not to poke yourself with it or the tube will be wasted - and you may hurt yourself," he instructed them, very firmly and as clearly as he could. They could see that he was being very serious.

"The aim of this game is to stick the sharp end of the tube into the leg or arm of the target I give to each of you, making sure to press it in hard. If you use enough force, the surface of the tube will turn red. If it doesn't do so, you won't have completed your task. Does everyone understand?" he asked.

All of them shook their heads - even Hung who was standing with the others, leaning on his crutch. Chien went through it again. It seemed very mysterious and exciting to the children - and on the face of it, there seemed to be little point to it, but they all knew that they mustn't ask questions:

what Chien wanted with the tubes after they had completed their tasks was none of their concern. They trusted him and if he wanted it done, then they would do it, whether it was for good or... not. Eventually, they all understood the outline - the essentials - of what was required of them.

Chien looked hard at Hung. He changed his mind about asking him. He decided that Hung wasnt well enough.

"Little Dragon, you're injured and you're excused from this exercise," Chien informed him. The other children smiled: this was the first time they had heard Chien call Hung "Little Dragon" and they liked it.

"I can do it, sir," Hung said, both slightly disappointed and worried at the same time. He did not want to be left out of anything, particularly if he might get something out of it which would be to his advantage.

"If you're sure?" Chien queried. Hung nodded, as did Chien in return.

Chien took them around the market and gave each of them their specific target to track - a total of four men. He provided each of the children with a plan of campaign, a method of tracking that he wanted them to adopt. When everyone appeared to understand what was expected of them and he was satisfied that they were ready, he signaled them to track down their targets.

Chien watched as the four young hunters spread out through the market area, each heading for their particular target. Each of them kept close to the walls of the buildings in order to try to be less visible. They ducked and dived, hiding behind people in the crowded and busy market area so that their targets would not spot that they were being followed.

Sen, seeing her target approaching, ducked under a cart and as he walked by, she struck him with her tube, in the calf of his leg, with a sharp jab. Jumping sideways, the man grabbed his calf before spotting blood on his leg where he had been stuck. Quickly he looked under the cart but saw nothing except the ground. Chien watched as Sen's target started to walk slowly around the corner of a building. Sen made her way back to Chien. Then the target began to sway, then stumble. He fell over, into a bush, out of sight.

Nhât crept slowly up behind his target and stabbed the point of his tube into the man's thigh. As with Sen's target, this man also grabbed his leg and spun around, looking for his attacker, just as Nhât ducked around behind the man, thus keeping out of the target's sight. This sort of thing was just what Nhât was used to doing when pick-pocketing.

Grinning, Nhât disappeared behind a nearby hut before the man turned back again. Nhât's target felt his leg and, finding that it was bleeding a little, wiped his hands off on a rag and began walking towards the nearest shop for water. As he stepped forward, he started to feel dizzy and stumbled over. Wiping his forehead with the same rag, he staggered over to a wooden bench where he sat down heavily, before taking a few deep breaths - then slid down sideways, as if he had suddenly fallen asleep.

Kim walked straight towards his target. Just before reaching him, Kim acted as if he had tripped, falling to the ground in front of the man. As he did so, he stuck the thin tube into the man's foot. Kim's target gave a short yelp, then kicked the boy to the side of the street before carrying on his way.

LITTLE DRAGON

Kim looked at the tube in his hand: he saw what Sen and Nhât had seen with their tubes; the outside of it was now red. He took off, running back to Chien. His target walked a few more paces, then started swaying and staggering to one side and then to the other, before going straight again for a few steps. He then stumbled into the bushes along the side of the road, where he gently and wearily fell over.

Hung hobbled down a narrow passageway before he reached his target. He then acted as if his crutch had slipped out from under him. Hung's target reacted quickly to help catch the boy, allowing Hung to fall into his arms. As he did so, Hung stabbed the point of his tube sharply and firmly into the back of the man's hand before withdrawing it and hiding it under his shirt. Hung noted that the tube had gone red.

His target winced and then helped Hung stand upright again. He made sure that Hung was stable on his feet and was able to move again before he turned around and started walking away. Pulling out a small piece of cloth, he started dabbing at the puncture mark that Hung had made on his hand, cursing gently under his breath as he did so. He too started swaying, then fell into a small group of people nearby, who immediately started asking him if he was all right. Hung hobbled his way back into the safety of the crowd as fast as he could and disappeared from sight.

Unbeknownst to the four children, each of the tubes had contained a small dose of general anaesthetic: enough to knock out the targets for a short while so that the kids could make their escape.

Chien was satisfied that all the targets had been successfully stabbed, sufficient for his purposes. What those purposes were, Hung and the others were never told. Only

LITTLE DRAGON

years later, when recalling these events, did Hung wonder what Chien had been up to: at the time he knew that it wasn't his place to know - or even to think about what had happened.

Chien pulled open his satchel and had each child drop his or her tube or syringe into it, inspecting each one to make sure he saw red - blood - on the sides. Hung dropped his last and Chien gave him a quick smile.

"Good job," Chien told him, seeing that Hung's leg had begun hurting him again.

Chien only had a small dose of the pain-relieving medicine left and the last dose he had given Hung would have to last a while yet: Hung would have to bear the pain for a bit longer before he could have any more.

"Now we go into the jungle and then cross over into the southern part of town. I have some business to do there. It won't take long. Then we can head back to the boat to get ready to head out to sea," Chien told them.

Dusk was well advanced when they got to the south side of town and arrived at the place to where Chien was heading. It was a medium sized building, slightly run down, but more strongly built than the surrounding merchants' huts that littered the marketplace.

Chien knocked on the front door with one tap, then walked in, guiding the children inside past him. They had entered a drinking house or bar. Once they were all in, Chien guided them over to one of three tables in the small kitchen which lay off to one side of the bar.

"If anyone else comes in, bang on the table a few times

just loud enough for me to hear through that door," Chien instructed them. "Understand?"

They all nodded. Chien waved to a lady standing behind the bar counter who brought each child a small dish of sweet cake with frosting, along with a small wooden fork.

"To the victors go the spoils," he said with a smile.

The children's eyes widened with excitement as they tucked into their reward. Chien slipped into the back room of the bar, carrying his satchel. Clearly, he had business to handle.

Hung and the other kids enjoyed the sweet taste of the treat but they were constantly scanning the room, looking out for anything out of place or anyone approaching. Once they had finished, they stacked up their dishes and forks neatly in the center of the table - customary when eating away from home - and wiped down the table. They waited quietly.

After a few moments, Chien returned from the back room. As he approached them, Hung noticed that Chien was carrying a different satchel to the one that he had taken into the back room. Hung was curious about the change - but knew enough not to ask.

Chien saw that everyone had finished their cake and had properly stacked the dishes and forks and cleaned the table in the way that he had taught them to be correct and proper. He gestured to the children to leave the bar. Standing up, they went outside into the fading light of dusk and the cooler air of the harbor, then made their way back to the shop.

The stars gradually came out, along with a full moon which

seemed to be observing them; watching over them as they walked along the familiar road. Trees, short and stout, lined the dirt road like guardian soldiers, as folk went home, about their business, or out for an evening's entertainment.

A short way along the road, Chien looked down at Hung, noticing that he was really struggling with the pain in his leg - although as was to be expected, Hung was not complaining. Chien squatted down on his haunches, he offered Hung a ride on his back - a piggyback.

"Hop up, Little Dragon, I'll get you there," Chien said with a smile.

Hung looked up at him. He couldn't believe what he had heard. His heart warmed: his mind was thinking this is just what a proper Dad would do. Handing his crutch to Nhât with a grin, he climbed up on Chien's back for the free ride.

"Thank you, sir," Hung said, climbing aboard with glee.

As he grabbed hold of Chien around his shoulders and neck, Hung slipped back a bit because of his bad leg. As he did so, something fell from his pocket onto the ground. Chien saw the glint from the metal cylinder as it hit the packed dirt path. He picked it up and slipped it into his pocket for later. Making sure Hung was holding on securely, he started forward again.

All four children were pretty much worn out. They were dragging ass as they trudged up to the entrance to Chien's shop, hoping they would be able to hit their hammocks straight away, ready for a good night's rest. Chien instructed them to put their things away and to hit the sack for some sleep. Walking over to Hung's hammock, he turned around and let Hung slide off directly into his hammock. Chien pulled another bottle from his pocket and handed it to him to drink down so he could sleep soundly through the night.

"Thank you sir," Hung said tiredly.

"You're very welcome, Hung. You did an excellent job today. You're a very strong and resourceful boy and have proven that today. I am proud of you." Chien rested his hand on the back of Hung's head.

"Now get some rest, Little Dragon, so you can heal up." There was a tone of deep caring in Chien's voice.

"Yes sir," Hung replied softly.

With that, Chien turned on his heel and walked out of the shop. He looked up above him, into the night, gazing at all the stars that blanketed the sky.

The sky reminded him of... Her.

He could still hear her voice in his head and see her beautiful face as she spoke to him. Tears started to run down his cheeks as he looked away from the sky and down to the ground. Wiping the tears away and shaking his head, his hands balled into fists.

Turning around, he walked down the dirt road back towards the marketplace, suddenly hearing her screaming in his head. He tried to make the screams go away - but they grew louder and louder the further he walked. On he went, the anger inside him building and building all the time until it took control of him.

CHAPTER ELEVEN

Opening the door to the tavern, Chien entered the place he knew a little too well. The heady jumble of smells - from food to sex - overpowered the senses, making his eyes water in smoky fug that filled the room. A racket of voices from all sides roared out together and clashed with each other, filling Chien's head with snippets of several different conversations at once. The hubbub was almost deafening.

He could hear her voice in his head fading as the clanging of pots and glasses rang out across the room. Lots of people were eating, drinking and conversing at the dozens of tables in the room.

His head began to hurt from the strain of keeping her screams out of his mind. He could feel the anger swelling as the thumping in his head got louder. Reaching into his satchel, he pulled out a few coins. He placed them on the bar and the barman traded them for a large jug of rice wine. Within a few seconds, Chien had tipped it up and downed its entire contents with the skill and speed of a hardened drinker.

He reached into the satchel again with the same result: the smiling barman refilled the jug. It was emptied as fast as the first. Her voice was becoming quieter... Reaching into the satchel again... The barman filling the jug for the third time... Her voice was even quieter now. It was being replaced, faintly, by the tune of a much-loved old song: one that meant a lot to them both; reminding him of special, happy, times. They seemed so long ago.

A fourth time - but this time the wine went down slower. Chien was swaying gently when he carefully and deliberately returned the jug to the bar counter. His head hurt from the strain but her voice was gone. The tune in his head was louder now. Although her voice had gone, the song made him think of... her - and what could have been. Tears ran down his face.

"Awww... Does the old man miss his mommy?"

A deep voice came from behind him. Then he heard a couple more voices chiming in and joining with the laughter that quickly followed. Chien's chest started to swell up with fury. He steadied himself and tried to stay calm and detached. Something was pulling at him... Don't react; that is what they are wanting you to do.

"What's the matter? Are you crying for me? Don't cry for me, old man!"

Chien remained still, clenching his fists by his sides, trying to stay in control of himself.

"Hey, why are you ignoring me, sissy man?"

He felt a hand grab his left shoulder, forcing him to turn around.

Chien let his body turn with the grip on his shoulder but as he did so, he swung his right arm in a sharp and powerful punch, his fist catching the man square on the chin with a loud crack and causing his head to spin to the right. Spit and teeth flew from the man's mouth.

As Chien turned, he brought his arm down in a vicious chop, hard onto the man's elbow. The man's arm went dead: it was useless to him, at least for a short while. Chien immediately followed up with a powerful punch with his left fist, straight into the man's solar plexus. The air flew from his lungs in a whoosh and the man staggered back. Chien followed and hit him with a vicious chop, with the blade of his right hand, straight onto the assailant's nose. He heard a most satisfying crack. The man fell flat on his back, unconscious.

Chien was starting to struggle: he was rapidly running out of energy. He swayed and stumbled back a couple of paces, partly from the violent movements of his attack and partly from the intoxication caused by the rice wine which was overpowering both his mind and balance. He felt fuzzy - out of it, detached. A heady combination when mixed with a burst of adrenaline.

He looked up only to see three other men coming towards him fast. They jumped on him like a pack of wild dogs. They threw him against one of the heavy, solid, tables. Unable to get his hands up in time to protect himself, one side of his face was slammed into the table, blurring his vision even more. Rolling onto his back, he looked up just in time to catch a fist on the other side of his face. Pain exploded through his head as the others started raining punches down on him until eventually darkness overcame him and he blacked out.

LITTLE DRAGON

Chien felt one arm being lifted and then the other as he started to regain consciousness. Immediately a coughing fit overcame him and he started hoicking out small gobs of blood, spit and snot as the children carefully lifted him up and started helping him along the road towards the harbor.

"The men must have dragged me out of the bar and left me on the edge of the marketplace," he thought to himself, slowly looking up at the sun. He was sufficiently alert to realize that it was almost midday. *"The children must have woken and come looking for me when I wasn't there for breakfast,"* he decided. *"STUPID!"* Chien was angry with himself. What a terrible example to set the children.

After several long rests along the way - and a couple of vomiting sessions - the children pulled Chien into the back of the shop at the harbor, lying him down carefully in his hammock. Hung hobbled off and then came back with some water which Chien choked down, accompanied by much coughing and spitting. He then lay back in his hammock. Nhât went over to the shelf on the side wall and, taking one of the last three small bottles of medicine that Chien had been giving Hung, emptied it into Chien's mouth before he slipped back into unconsciousness.

…"Don't go," he pleaded with her. "It's too dangerous: this hasn't been thought through properly. It's a badly planned operation, even for the Resistance. And you know it."

"You know I have to. They're not giving me any choice," she explained.

"We can take the boat out to sea and simply disappear," he pleaded with her.

LITTLE DRAGON

"They have every harbor watched and they would kill us both for being deserters. It would be treason!" she replied.

He could see he wasn't winning the argument. When all was said and done, she was right and he knew it.

In his unconscious state, Chien shook his head from side to side, trying to wake himself up, knowing what was coming next.

He could hear her calling for him. He can't find a way in. Another scream... He shook his head harder... "Wake up!" he tried to yell to himself. No good...

He started to shake his head even harder, slamming it one way and then the other. The screams faded... They faded further... And then even more...

They were gone. Gone... For the moment.

Chien opened his eyes. Hung was wiping Chien's sweating forehead with a wet rag. On a small table alongside the hammock, Hung set a small tray of fish and crab meat, along with more water and one of the last two bottles of medicine. Hung turned, heading out the back door to see to the rest of his chores. Chien could hear the others rustling about, doing their chores and chatting with each other to decide what still needed to be done and who was going to do it.

"What amazing children these are," he thought to himself, sitting up enough so as to grab the tray. He started to eat slowly, trying to regain some strength.

He looked over to his shelving unit where he kept his personal belongings. He saw his satchel hanging on the coat hook. Chien gave a long, deep sigh of relief. At least he hadn't got himself robbed at the bar. That would have been disastrous, what with all they had ahead of them.

Chien finished the food and took his medicine. Gradually, he started to feel stronger. He could feel the pain from all the bruising starting to reduce as the medicine entered his bloodstream, soothing the nerve endings.

Slowly, he leaned over out of the hammock and planted his feet as firmly as he could on the floor, giving his body time to adjust and to respond to his commands. His muscles objected painfully to the tasks they were being told to do and it took a lot longer for them to be ready for him to move.

Standing up and with several cracks and pops from the joints in his body, Chien gave a stifled groan: all the muscles in his back and chest that had been beaten up hit him with a rolling wave of pain. He closed his eyes and tried to focus for a second. After a few moments, he regained his composure and opened his eyes again. After what Hung had been through, Chien wanted to show to Hung - and the others - the same strength.

Staggering out to the front of the shop, Chien tried not to act like his legs didn't want to work. He peered past the shop counter to the quayside: he could see Kim and Sen loading supplies onto High Tides while Nhât was busy gutting and cleaning fish and crabs from a net. Clearly, he had been fishing from the beach. All of them were pitching in and carrying out their tasks, allotted or not, in unison for the good of the group. To Chien's eyes, it was nothing short of perfect. He had a troop - a proper family. He felt quite emotional. Tears came to his eyes.

LITTLE DRAGON

He was aware that he was going to be taking the children to a dangerous place. Any of them could be seriously injured or even killed by animals, hunters or any number of dangers that lurk in the jungle's hidden recesses, but for the sake of all of them, they still had to go with him. He needed to get hold of particular plants and flowers which he knew could only be found there.

There were other things there that he needed to get his hands on - but he couldn't tell the kids what they were. They must never know the details of what he was up to. It was a huge risk. The children would need more training - very specific and targeted training - mostly about what to avoid, to help them be on their guard where they were going next. Not that the sea itself was any less forgiving to boats than what they would experience where they would be heading.

These kids had become special to him. He watched them, all working hard to do their part for the team. Chien looked around: the only child he couldn't see was Hung who was the one he was the most concerned about, particularly with his leg being in its current condition. Chien walked up behind Nhât, who was just finishing gutting the fish. Nhât put the last of the scraps into a basket which he was picking up, ready for loading onto the junk.

"Where's Hung?" Chien asked suddenly.

Nhât straightened up so quickly that he almost lost balance. He dropped the basket, throwing all over the ground the fish scraps he had just gathered up.

"Damn! Every time! He does that to me every time!" Nhât whispered to himself under his breath as he turned around to see Chien with the biggest grin on his face. Nhât could swear

that Chien was going to bust out laughing at any moment.

"He insisted that he be the one to look after the market shop, so he headed back there right after he checked on you," Nhât answered, his slight irritation at being startled again showing a little. He then crouched down to start picking up the fish scraps.

"Very well. Carry on," Chien replied sarcastically, but with an undertone of gentle teasing.

Chien then set off, walking down the road. Very slowly.

Halfway along his walk to the marketplace, Chien saw Hung coming along the road towards him, heading back to the harbor, using his crutch with skill so that he was making steady progress. However, Chien could see that something was bothering Hung. Hung raised his eyes from the road: he could see Chien walking towards him, so he sped up as much as the crutch would allow him.

"You didn't have to come, sir. I was OK." Hung looked up at Chien, happy he had come anyway.

"I am sure you were," said Hung. "I didn't expect to see you coming back so early." He was questioning Hung - sort of - even though he was happy that he didn't have to make the full trip back to the marketplace, despite Hung having just done it.

"Well..." Hung said, looking at the ground.

"What's wrong?" Chien pressed him

"I really didn't see any reason to stay longer at the shop, sir.

LITTLE DRAGON

The number of bodies from the refugee boats that have been washing up along the coastline near the harbor is getting too great for the harbor authority to clear quickly.

"It's like the whole town is down at the harbor entrance and along the shoreline, trying to drag the bodies out of the sea. No one was at the market to buy anything. I've been down near the beach: people are flat out pulling bodies out of the water. They're stacking them along the shore. They are saying one of the larger ships must have sunk or capsized and dumped everyone in the water," Hung explained, continuing to fix his eyes firmly on the ground.

Chien could tell that the images of what Hung had seen on the beach would not leave his mind or imagination any time soon.

"Yes, Little Dragon, it is grim... Horrible," Chien said, resting his hand gently on Hung shoulder. "I guess we should head back to the boat before we're blocked in as well."

Chien knew the tide would be coming in, so they wouldn't have very long to wait before it would be bringing more bodies in with it, back towards the harbor entrance. If that happened, it could be days before the authorities would allow them to sail, as they were likely to close the harbor.

No boats would be allowed to enter or leave while the harbor staff were dealing with all the bodies. Particularly so now that the staff were extremely busy, working at their regular job of digging out and clearing the channel leading into the harbor - on top of the additional revolting task of fishing grisly, stinking, corpses from the sea. The recovery and proper disposal of the bodies would take days after that. Chien could not wait that long: he had to set sail with this tide and somehow steer clear of the next incoming wave of gut-churningly rotten human flesh.

"We must get back quickly and load everything onto the boat as fast as possible," Chien said, turning on his heel and starting to walk back to High Tides, at the same time urging Hung to speed up as much as he could.

Back at the harbor, the first thing Chien did was to call the children together and thank them for the care and support they had all shown him as he had been recovering from being beaten up. He made it clear to them that they had all done well, that he was proud of them and that they should be proud of themselves.

He didn't say anything about how or why he had got drunk in the first place. As ever, the children knew not to ask. If Chien wanted them to know anything more, they knew that he would tell them in his own time.

Time was marching on: Chien began directing the children like the leader of an orchestra, waving his arms around in all directions. They followed his instructions to the letter. Weaving around each other as if in a dance, loading supplies and equipment onto the deck and breaking out the sail ready for casting off.

Chien picked up the last two bottles of medicine and what herbs he had left from the store and was putting them into his pocket when he found inside it the small silver cylinder that had fallen from Hung's pocket as he had given Hung the piggyback. He looked at it closely. He had forgotten all about it until now. However seeing it again, it finally dawned on him what it was, once he got a close look.

"Hung!" he exclaimed, raising his voice above his normally quiet and measured tone for extra urgency.

After a moment, Hung appeared in front of him, slightly red in the cheeks and a bit out of puff. He had noticed the unusual, for Chien, tone in the call and so had rushed as fast as he could to get to him.

"Yes sir?" he enquired politely.

"Where did you get this?" Chien began. "Do you have any more of them?" he asked

I have a few more left in the pack with the rest of the stuff that came with them." Hung answered.

"Make sure you grab all you have, along with the other bits and pieces that you found with them. It's essential that you bring all of it. OK?" Chien said, looking Hung straight in the eye. He wanted to impress upon Hung the importance of what he was saying.

"Yes sir," Hung replied. He limped over to his hammock: he kept what was left of the pack underneath it.

Chien looked towards the sea. He could see that the incoming tide was carrying yet more bodies. He could see many dark, macabre, waves of rotting flesh approaching them slowly. The floating dead. Many bodies had been partially eaten by sharks and even the sea birds were pecking at the corpses. It was like a horror movie. He knew that they didn't have more than another hour before the influx of bodies drifting towards the harbor entrance would mean that they would not be able to get away.

LITTLE DRAGON

Rushing the children along, Chien felt his body start to weaken from the combined strain of all the work he had been doing for the past months and years, as well as being beaten up so severely. He pushed himself to carry on.

At last they all clambered aboard the junk, carrying the last of the supplies that they had brought down from the shop with them. Chien unfurled the sail and dropped the mooring ropes from the dockside. There was hardly any breeze so everyone grabbed oars and started to paddle. As they did so, bodies began bumping up against the surrounding boats in the harbor - the first of the latest stream of bodies that were arriving on the incoming tide.

Chien did the best he could to steer High Tides away from the parts of the harbor where the tide was washing in the majority of dead bodies. They began to hear the thumps of heads bouncing off the hulls of the ships. The sheer number of bodies was overwhelming the harbor authorities - and now the townsfolk too.

They strained to paddle around the bodies until finally, a kindly current began to pull them out into deeper water, away from the gruesome sights. A combination of the sea and gentle breeze slowly carried them out into the approaching night, away from the waves of death along the shoreline and away from the flames of the funeral pyres that were cremating the bodies which had already been pulled from the sea.

They were in open waters but kept the coastline in sight for the time being, until Chien and the children had been able to start bringing some sort of order and organization to the junk. In all the excitement, Chien had forgotten that this was Hung's first time on the junk - or any "proper" boat for all he knew.

He could see Hung looking around, admiring the craftsmanship. High Tides was not a small junk, but not especially large either. However, it seemed spacious enough for the five of them and all their supplies and they would still be able to walk about on deck comfortably. Once all the supplies had been stowed away in their proper places, the deck would be open and there would be plenty of room for all of them.

"Hung and Nhât: come with me," Chien called out to them, having first locked the wheel to a fixed course. He pointed towards a hatch set into the superstructure of the High Tides.

The two boys followed Chien through the doorway. It led to six steps down to a short passageway, about five or six meters long, which had two doors on both sides, close together. In addition, there was another door at the end of the passageway, which had a small shield above it. On the shield were the words: "High Tides". Her name was on the bow, on both sides, and below deck. About halfway along the corridor, there was a trapdoor set into the floor. The trapdoor had the word "Storage" carved into it.

"First door to the left is the mess cabin with a small galley. That's the kitchen area on a boat and I use it both for preparing meals and cleaning fish," Chien started, pointing to the door he was referring to. "First door on the right is for dry storage and medical supplies - things that mustn't get wet."

"Second door on the right is the boys' cabin and sleeping quarters." Chien opened that door and pointed to their bunks. "You two and Kim will sleep there.

"Second door on the left is Sen's cabin and some extra storage." He waved in the direction of Sen's cabin. "The last door at the end is the Captain's quarters where I sleep."

With that, he pulled out a key from a pouch that was fixed to his belt and unlocked the Captain's cabin door. He led the two boys into the cabin. To the back of the room was a small desk and chair that sat in front of two large windows. These windows looked out over the stern of the boat, so Chien could see what was happening behind them. Just under the windows were small shelves upon which were various items which had been secured firmly so that they would not move with the motion of the junk. On each of the adjoining side walls of the cabin was a single window, thus giving the Captain a good view from all sides of High Tides, except for the bow.

In addition, each wall of the cabin was lined with various homemade wooden racks that held rifles and handguns of various calibers and from different makers. Below those were cabinets and drawers that had also been fastened to the walls and which had latches, allowing them to be closed firmly and also locked. Their contents were hidden. Spear racks were fastened to the wall on both sides of the entrance door. One spear in each slot of the racks; four spears in each rack. A total of eight.

High Tides had been built to look like a fishing junk or trawler but was much sturdier and stronger and quite a bit wider than most such ships, in order to provide more space for smuggling goods. The hull had been built deeper to take even more illegal cargo, but this also meant that she could not sail in waters that were relatively shallow. Her solid construction made sure that High Tides could absorb a fierce attack. She would have to be on the receiving end of a good many shells and suffer heavy structural damage before she would be at risk of sinking.

LITTLE DRAGON

And as a last resort, Chien knew that he could, if necessary, just turn her straight towards his enemy and ram the son of a bitch - High Tides was that sturdy. Chien really did love this junk: his pride and joy. It had saved his life more times than he could remember - not that he wanted to dwell on those thoughts.

Chien watched the boys gazing around his cabin in amazement, like kids in a toy store wanting to play. He let them look around as he made his way to the Captain's chair and sat down, giving his body a much-needed rest. As he sank into the comfort of the chair, his muscles seemed to give a collective sigh of thanks, expressed by a long, contented exhaling of breath.

"I shall train you boys in as many of the weapons that you see as I can," Chien said to them. Hung and Nhât were amazed - and thrilled.

Chien waved his arm at the collection of weapons that was spread around the cabin. There were rifles, handguns and machetes of every description and size.

"Where we are going to now is where I found all of these, save one. It will be extremely dangerous and you must always follow my instructions completely and do exactly as you are told AT ONCE, or we could all be killed. Death could find any of us in any number of different ways - all painful. None would be quick or painless."

Chien deliberately made the point as forcefully as he could: he wanted it to lodge firmly in the boys' minds now - before the real action started. Kim and Sen had had his lecture before - more than once - and he knew from how they had responded that they had got the message. He was concerned to make sure that Hung and Nhât understood, particularly since they were a bit older and, because of their tough backgrounds, probably thought they were more street-wise and savvy than they were.

"Yes, sir " Hung spoke up first.

"Yessir," Nhât followed up.

"Now, go help the others take care of the stowage of the rest of the supplies and then you can hit the sack for some rest. We will be sailing a while before we get to where we are going."

The boys turned, walking out of the cabin obediently. Chien slumped down into his chair, knowing there was so much more to do.

An hour passed and everything had been stowed away in its proper place. All four children were in their cabins. Chien stood at the bow of his ship, staring up at the full moon, which seemed to stare back at him, with all its stars surrounding it. He breathed in deeply the salty air, appreciating the absence of the horrible stench of burning and rotting bodies that otherwise would stay in his nostrils for days. Out here, away from everything and everyone, he could find his center: the last remaining impression of peace left to him. His boat and the sea.

"Hello, Little Dragon," Chien said, sensing that he was being watched from behind.

Hung couldn't believe he knew he was there. He had been so quiet. Hung couldn't get over the fact that seemingly no one had ever been able to startle Chien. Ever. That was just not right.

"Hello, sir. I will go back to my bunk," Hung replied.

"Come here, Hung." Chien waved him to come alongside him.

"I have a feeling that you will not find such peace as this again for some time, so enjoy it while you can." Chien went on: "It's all the little enjoyments and pleasures which, when put together, make life wonderful and worth the time and energy we use to live it to the fullest."

"I understand, sir."

"Yes, I know you do, Hung. You are an exceptional boy," Chien complimented Hung. Hung held his tongue briefly, not knowing what to say to such a compliment.

"Thank you, sir," was all he could think to say at that moment.

"I have seen that the way you do any one thing is the way you do everything. That is what makes you stand out. Never lose that," Chien complimented Hung again.

"Someday I swear I'm gonna be a famous movie star or someone rich and if I can't do that then I'll be a gangster!" Hung started blurting out all of a sudden. "I'll be the biggest gangster ever and won't take shit from no one. I'll have so much money, I'll save us all and we'll never need money again!"

Hung stopped, having run out of puff. He had made his declaration in one go, without taking a breath. He wasn't sure why he had said it. Chien just grinned, mainly to himself.

"What sort of boy - what sort of man - was he making out of Hung?" he asked himself.

For the next hour, they both stood there, side by side, on the bow of the High Tides, breathing in the cool night air. Neither spoke: they were both lost in their thoughts. The only sounds were the waves gently slapping the bow as it sliced through the sea like a sharp knife through butter, the occasional creak of the rigging and soft flapping of the sail above their heads.

The gentle rocking of the junk and soothing sounds of the waves began to have their effect upon Hung. Tiredness was catching up with him and calling him back to sleep, so he said good night to Chien and headed for his bunk. As he entered through the hatch to head for his cabin, he took one last look over his shoulder at Chien standing at the bow. Then he went below.

Chien stayed on deck for a while longer. He knew that this would be the last period of relatively calm and peace that he - or the children - would experience for some time. He wanted to make the most of it. The melody that had come into his head when he was in the bar started up in his head again. Faintly at first, but gradually louder. Not so that he felt overwhelmed by it, but enough for him to start humming and then singing along with it. Gently - almost in a whisper. *Lan và Điệp:* that was the song. He and she had sung it together. It had been their song.

This time the song didn't cause any tears. He felt sad, yes. But now the memories were mainly the good ones. He missed her so much, but he felt that he should remember the happy times rather than the sad ones.

CHAPTER TWELVE

Hung woke to a series of sharp knocks on the cabin door. The other two boys jerked awake too and all three of them sat up straight away and hurried as fast as they could to get ready to go up on deck. Hung clambered off his bunk and, noticing his leg was feeling a little better, put his foot flat on the cabin floor and applied pressure to it. His leg gave him a little pain, but it was much more tolerable than yesterday, so he left the crutch where it was. He was still walking with a slight limp, but it was better not having to use the crutch any more. He felt free again.

Chien was out on the open deck. He saw Hung walking without the use of the crutch and gave him a nod of approval. Hung smiled back. Chien had set up a small table which was laid out with large heavy bowls that would not tip with the swaying of the junk. They all sat and ate their breakfast as High Tides carried them steadily onwards towards their destination. Chien looked weary from keeping watch while the children had slept, so he gave Kim their current heading and instructed him to maintain the same course while he got some rest. Chien locked the wheel to the set course and headed to his cabin.

Kim and Sen started to tell Nhât and Hung the list of daily duties and chores that had to be carried out while on board. Kim decided who would do what: no arguments from the others as they knew that Kim was the most experienced of the four of them when it came to sailing. When Kim had sorted out the jobs, each of them knuckled down to work.

They worked hard and with enthusiasm: just as well as there seemed to be a lot to be done. Kim kept finding them something else to do, but they didn't mind; they wanted to get High Tides as shipshape as they could for Chien.

It took them longer than they had expected, but during the morning they were able to get through a lot of the jobs. Around midday, Sen took Hung to a quieter part of the deck and spent some time trying to teach him how to read and write - which he found to be quite a struggle.

When Sen had finished giving her lesson, the boys headed to the galley and started prepping for a late lunch. Chien came up on deck shortly after, looking very much rested. He never seemed to need much sleep in order to replenish his energy tanks.

As soon as the food was ready they sat together and ate, thankful that the voyage, up to now at least, had been "So Far, So Good". When their bellies were full, they cleared up the dishes and bowls and got back to finishing their chores. Hung had moved up to the bow of the ship to lash down a few barrels more securely and was hard at work again when Chien stepped up behind him.

"Little Dragon."

"Yes, sir."

"I want to speak to you about a few things."

LITTLE DRAGON

"OK," Hung said, sitting down on a crate and giving Chien his undivided attention.

"The night you found me on the road near the marketplace, beaten up and drunk: I wanted to try to explain the reason behind my stupid actions which caused you to find me that way."

"OK, sir," was all Hung said. He wasn't sure where Chien was going with this and he didn't want to offend him by sounding cocky, having witnessed what clearly Chien saw as being a weakness in himself. He felt that Chien didn't need to explain himself but if by telling him, that would help Chien, then so be it.

Chien spoke quietly for a long time about a past life - far more dangerous than his current life - and more dangerous than that of any of the four children too. He told Hung of a secret army that had recruited him a long time ago, at a time when the Americans came to take over the country, at the same time pretending to be supporters of their cause.

Chien had used this very boat to smuggle anything and everything, back and forth, from north to south - weapons, information and sometimes even people. Now Hung really understood why this ship meant so much to Chien and why he kept it in good repair in the way he did.

One of Chien's missions had been to smuggle a young and pretty girl: an agent - a spy - into an American military camp, disguised as a prostitute so that she could gather information about intended targets that the Americans were treating as Viet Cong hot-spots and which the USAF were preparing to bomb. The aim had been to give the Viet Cong as much warning as possible so that their troops and armaments could be moved before the bombing raids. Chien had picked up the agent at the appointed rendezvous and helped smuggle her onto the American base. Then over the next several years, the two of them had worked together regularly, becoming close and then intimate on several occasions: they had become a couple. Kim was the son they had together. Kim sailed with Chien from a very early age, as the girl was working undercover for long periods of time. The name of the pretty girl - Kim's mother - was Tien.

One day, Tien was captured by an American scouting party. She was brought back to their base of operations, where for several days, she had been tortured for information about those she was working with. Chien had waited outside the base for her return, unaware of what was happening inside the security fence. Chien hadn't been expecting to meet up with her for a few days, so he wasn't particularly worried about her for a while.

During the night after Tien failed to return as expected, Chien tried penetrating the base himself to find her. Under the cover of darkness, upon getting close to the fence around the camp, he could hear her screaming as she was being tortured. He had moved around to the front gate of the base and just as he got there, the gate swung open with a loud crash. He melted back into the shadows as he saw several men exit the gate and throw someone to the ground.

"Useless bitch!" one of them yelled at her, kicking dirt into her face then turning away. The soldiers went back inside the base.

As soon as they were out of sight, Chien ran over to her and carried her back to High Tides as quickly as he could. He set up a make-do medical table to lay her upon, in order to assess her injuries.

Tien's face had several fractures and most of her teeth had been knocked out - not that you'd notice straight away, since her face had been badly beaten up and was heavily scarred. One eye was so swollen as to be completely closed and the other had blood running from it. Some of her fingers were missing and most of the others were either broken or dislocated. Her left arm was broken, along with several ribs.

He knew she didn't have long to live from the way she was spitting up so much blood. There must have been even more internal injuries which Chien knew he could not get to. And even if he did, there was nothing that he could do to save her.

She stopped him from inspecting her injuries. She smiled at him the best she could. She didn't have much energy left but she lifted the arm which was slightly less injured than the other and, putting her broken fingers against his cheek, told him to listen.

Tien then told him of their daughter, Sen. She had been born in the town nearest to the American military base: Tien could not risk breaking her cover as a prostitute and she carried on with her work throughout her pregnancy and after Sen was born. Until that moment, Chien did not know that he had a daughter: Tien had been working undercover and he had been sailing up and down the coast, smuggling, for so long. Kim had a sister!

Tien told Chien that Sen was waiting for him to fetch her so that she could be with her brother and father. Tien told him of the friend who was looking after Sen and where to find her. As she finished, her lungs filled with blood and she died.

LITTLE DRAGON

Looking up at Chien, Hung saw him in a very different light. Without saying anything, Hung got up and gave Chien a big hug, knowing that enough words had been spoken for now.

Both of them were wrapped up in their own thoughts. Time passed. Neither of them spoke; they were both letting their minds wander. Remembering times past. For Chien, the soft tune of Lan và Điệp came back to him again. This time, even though he had just told Hung of the horrors that had happened to Tien, the song brought no sad memories; just the happier ones.

Eventually, they were brought out of their dreamings by the calls of birds flying overhead. Daylight was starting to fade. Stars were appearing in the darkening sky.

"Land is close. We are nearing our journey's end," Chien informed him. "We will have to drop anchor soon and wait for the morning light; it will be way too dangerous for you and the other children in the dark. Anyway, I'll be able to scout out the area in the morning, before bringing the four of you ashore." After hearing the story he just heard, Hung was more than satisfied with that.

The heat of the day crept quickly into the boys' cabin the following morning. Sweat trickled down the side of Hung's face, waking him. He looked over and saw that Nhât and Kim were already up, getting ready for the morning chores and breakfast. Hung's stomach gave a growl at the thought of food. Yup: he could definitely eat!

LITTLE DRAGON

He slid out of his bunk, onto the floor. He noticed that the pain in his leg was almost gone: thank heavens he was a fast healer. With all the beatings over the years, it wasn't surprising that his body had adapted to repair itself quickly - it had to!

The boys hurried out through the cabin door. All three of them banged loudly on Sen's door on their way up onto the deck. She yelled back at them after each knock that she was coming. They reached the deck with Sen close behind, but Chien was not there - he was nowhere to be seen.

"Is he still in his cabin?" Sen asked.

"I don't think so," Kim replied.

"No, there he is." Nhât pointed out over the starboard side.

Coming up alongside High Tides was Chien in the canoe which Hung had noticed, before they left the harbor, had been strapped to the side of the junk. Chien signaled them to climb down into the canoe. They clambered aboard and then headed over to the island that lay in front of them.

The island looked lush and green. The trees that grew on its slopes were swaying a little in the fresh onshore breeze. Paddling towards the beach, they could hear the calls and sounds of animals and birds, hidden from sight.

At first glance, it was almost idyllic - a paradise. However, the closer they got to the island, the less welcoming it started to appear. What started as shoals of fish swimming in and around the forests of sea kelp soon turned into a few stragglers - fish that had become separated from the main shoal - darting nervously in and out between large chunks of metal debris, jumbled up with the rotting timber and other flotsam from wrecked boats. There even seemed to be what looked like a few bones here and there. At that point, Hung stopped looking in the water.

As they approached the beach, they noticed something strange about the coastal strip of land: it was covered with a lot of strange mounds of earth and long trenches, some of which had been dug out of the sand and others in the soil of the thin strip of open ground in front of the jungle.

Trees had been cut down in great numbers in some places and nearby were large stacks of torn sandbags, mixed in with other bags and rubbish, all of which seemed to be rotting slowly into the ground. Hung was starting to get the feeling that he really didn't want to be here, but it was too late to go back: the canoe hit the sand of the beach and stopped.

Chien climbed out of the canoe first, grabbing as he got up the two backpacks that were sitting in front of him. He shouldered one and gave the other to Nhât who was getting out next. Once they were all ashore, Chien picked up the rope that was fixed to the front of the canoe and tied it off onto a tree a short distance above the beach.

"I'm leaving out an extra long length of rope so the canoe stays floating out in the water. I do this to reduce the risk of animals getting into the canoe and also to stop anything else on the beach - such as sharp rocks or other things - damaging it," he explained to them. He liked teaching his young crew in this way, better than any other. The kids could see clearly for themselves not only what he was doing, but also why.

Chien signaled everyone to come in close and to hunker

down around him. They huddled around in a tight circle, facing each other - and waited.

"Whenever possible, we should always stay low like this, especially when talking amongst ourselves and moving around," Chien began.

"Are there other people here, sir?" Nhât asked, wondering who could possibly want to be here.

"Ahh, that is the big question," Chien replied. "If we don't know - and we don't - then the best thing to do is to assume that there are and to make sure you see them first. If we stay low and together like this, we are less at risk of being spotted or losing one another.

"Do you understand?" he asked them, looking for a nod of acceptance from each of them - which he got straight away.

"Do you see the red flags marking out the area around us?" Chien pointed out the boundaries of a large stretch of beach and foreshore that surrounded them. There were flags sticking up out of the sand at regular intervals, forming a large and unmistakable perimeter. He saw the children scan the area and then each of them said either "Yes, sir" or "Yes, Dad".

"Good. The most important rule is to not go outside those flags unless I am with you. Everything inside should be fairly safe because I have already checked over this area while you were sleeping, before I came back to the boat. However, that does not mean that it is completely safe so no one goes anywhere alone. Understood?"

They all nodded their understanding and agreement.

LITTLE DRAGON

"There are many different kinds of creatures here, most of which are either very poisonous or venomous or ready to eat you, so keep your mind on your surroundings and your wits about you at all times. This is a dangerous place, in many ways. Knowing your surroundings out here will save your life."

In front of them were vast stretches of thick jungle, while away to both sides was more beach and open ground.

"Straight ahead down there" - Chien pointed along the beach to the south - "is a long trench that I cleared out before I marked the perimeter. It has a few wider places in it. We'll put our packs in a wide section and we'll make a campsite there to work from."

Chien half stood up and walked forward slowly, all the time examining thoroughly the ground in front and to the sides of him for signs of any changes since the last time he was here. One by one, the children stood up and followed his lead, keeping low as he had told them until they all came to a particularly long trench that had been dug out of the sand. This was just one of a large number of similar trenches that the kids could see, stretching off into the distance along the beach.

"Be careful in these trenches. The soldiers who dug them would set traps in them and in the small shelter holes that they prepared in lots of places, all over the island, particularly along the route of regularly used paths and on all the beaches. They hoped that others would fall into them. I've marked the traps that I have found, but I'm not perfect and may have missed some.

"I'll be showing you how to build and use these traps to

our advantage, both for catching animals and also to protect our campsite. You'll see that along the edge of some of the trenches are ladders for getting in and out of them quickly."

Chien was urging them to learn as much as they could, as quickly as possible: they listened intently, hanging on every word.

"Climb down that ladder over there," Chien said, "and we'll make camp in this trench. Prepare a fire pit in the center and set up two torches on either side of the trench, three or four feet out from the sides. Make sure to top them up with oil so they don't burn out during the night. At night, it's animals, not people, we need to be more concerned about. If there are people around, they'll come towards the torches - but we won't be sleeping near them."

That statement told them that they were staying the night out here on the beach - in the trench. For some reason, that didn't sound like fun to any of them.

The four children clambered down the rather shaky ladder and made quick work of setting up the camp. They tried to ready themselves for what might come next - not that they knew as yet what that would be.

Chien reached into his pack and pulled out three metal sections of what Hung and the others rapidly realized were the pieces of a rifle. Quickly and expertly, Chien assembled it.

"This is your standard enemy rifle. It's a single shot infantryman's rifle with a bayonet clip. It was used by thousands and thousands of soldiers. It's a very powerful rifle and will kill almost anything with a single shot if it hits the target in the right spot.

"The weakness, the snag, with this weapon is that after one shot you must reload and even with much practice, that can take several seconds. It also kicks like a horse which takes some getting used to."

Chien paused, then picked up a small bundle of bamboo poles which they had brought from the boat. He slung them over his shoulder and then climbed part of the way up the ladder on the south side of the trench and looked over the lip to see if there was any living thing- particularly any harmful thing - out there. He saw nothing so climbed out completely, carrying the rifle.

Raising the butt of the rifle to his shoulder, he looked along the barrel, checking its sights. He started to move forward slowly, crouching low, scanning from left to right repeatedly.

He went about a hundred meters out from the trench where he stopped and stabbed three of the poles into the sand. To each of the poles he attached a large target - driftwood from the beach. The targets were about five feet off the ground. Once he had all three targets secured, he made his way back to the trench and told the four of them to come up.

"Hung, step over here," Chien instructed Hung. He did so. He had Hung face towards the targets he had set up.

Chien moved up behind Hung and carefully positioned Hung's hands on the rifle in the correct places, showing him how to hold it, both for use and for safety. Hung had to stretch a bit to fix his hands where he was being shown. He found the rifle was very heavy. Chien put his hand on the bolt of the rifle and, pulling it back to show Hung how to open the chamber and where to put in the round, pointed to the round that was already loaded into the rifle.

"Once the round is in the chamber, push the bolt forward and then push the lever down to lock it. It's then ready to fire. Make sure the butt of the rifle, this bigger section, is firm against your shoulder because it's going to kick back hard against your body when you fire it. Line up the front point which is sticking up above the end of the barrel with the groove in the gun-sight and then onto the target. When you've done that, take a deep breath, then exhale and fire."

Hung took his time lining up the rifle - not really wanting to fire it. But once he had done so, he squeezed the trigger. A tremendous BANG rang out as the recoil of the shot pushed the rifle back into his shoulder.

Pain shot through the right side of his body, causing him to lose his grip on the weapon so that it flew out of his hands. The bolt and lever slammed into his cheek and bloodied his nose. Hung cried out - more from shock and surprise than pain. Chien just laughed briefly.

"Yup: that's what happened to me too, the first time," Chien said. Hung kept rubbing his face, hoping the pain would go away soon.

During the following days, the children were taught many skills by Chien. He was a strict taskmaster: they all spent long hours, listening, watching and then trying out what they had been taught - learning the practical skills of survival.

Chien showed each of the children the various weapons that Hung and Nhât had first seen in the Captain's cabin and, more to the point, how to use them. They all learned a lot -

and they learned fast.

Chien was an excellent and painstaking teacher, but he also drove the children hard: he was desperate that they learn as much as possible. Not only were they shown how to fire the rifle, but also to clean and care for it. And their lessons were not limited to the rifle: Chien brought automatic pistols and some of the other guns off High Tides and taught all of them how to use those weapons.

He showed them how to make and set various types of traps. Traps made with wire. Traps made with thin ropes. Others by digging holes in the sand, then concealing the holes without the thin surface collapsing in on itself. Traps made with razor-sharp bamboo sticks - these were spike traps. He went over with them the various ways and means of hunting and how to lead prey - both animals and birds, and even lizards, into the traps.

He taught them how to conceal themselves, both from human enemies and from dangerous animals. He showed them many of the poisons that they might come across - poisonous plants, berries, trees. Venomous snakes and other creatures. What plants and wildlife they could eat and what they must avoid - and ways to slow down the effects of those poisons.

He instructed them in the use of the machete. How to swing it in an attack - also how to use it efficiently and effectively in cutting through undergrowth, trees and bushes: in other words, how to force a path through the virtually impassable jungle that surrounded them above the beach line.

The children found it physically exhausting work; fighting their way through the jungle as fast as they could, learning how to work as a team, taking it in turns so that one of them would lead and cut away at the trees, branches, vines and huge leaves to clear a narrow path for all of them - with another of the children taking over as the one in the front became exhausted.

His lessons continued about the plants to pick for healing purposes: Chien was anxious that the children learn how to identify the medicinal plants so that if they spied any, they could collect them for him. These were the very flowers and plants that made up the painkiller that Hung was taking.

Above all, he taught them Special Operations skills and tactics. In particular how to move across the land - in the jungle, across open ground and on the beach - without making a sound. Stealth was of the utmost importance. How to camouflage yourself against whatever the background might be - trees, buildings, open ground... He showed them how to use stealth and cunning to deceive the enemy and catch them unaware. They were required by Chien to practice stealth, creeping up behind each other when they thought that one of them wasn't watching or wasn't paying attention.

The ultimate test started, however, when Chien ordered them to try and get up behind Chien himself, without him spotting them. The results of these attempts were "mixed" - at least to begin with - although they improved after much practice.

Hung and Nhât especially appreciated these lessons: ever since they had met him, they had been amazed by and in awe of Chien's rather spooky ability to come up behind them, even when they were out in the open, without them noticing him being there.

In effect, during that period, Chien was teaching the children the arts of guerilla warfare.

On top of all the teaching and training, the five of them hunted and trapped many animals and birds - plus the odd lizard - both for their skins and as food for the pot. Chien showed the children how to kill and skin their catches, how to cut them up and store them in salt for preservation.

All the animals they came across were small rodent types which were relatively easy to butcher and pickle in salty water for stowage on board. Hung became skilled at snaring and butchering lemurs which they trapped in the trees. Nhât proved to be quite the marksman, shooting lots of pheasants.

Potentially this could be a profitable skill: there were many merchants in the towns along the coast who would like to buy the birds' feathers for added decoration to go on smart clothes.

Chien encouraged the kids to play Hide and Seek. A childish game, of course, particularly in light of the training that they were getting in lethal skills, but valuable to Chien: by doing so, it meant that, while looking for whoever was hiding, they were searching a large part of the island. They found many abandoned or lost supply drop sites which had either been forgotten about or which had become of no use to those setting them up, perhaps due to the fighting in the war moving on, across to other islands.

They found, dug out and dragged down to the camp in the trench, boxes of guns, grenades, ammunition and explosives. Weapons of every description: 9mm handguns, machine guns, automatics and more rifles. Also, they discovered large quantities of unexploded bombs that had been dropped but which proved to be duds. They always steered clear of those.

As ever the children knew not to ask Chien any questions about what he wanted with what they were finding: "Don't ask, don't tell" was always their motto. However, from things that Chien told them over the weeks they were together, soon all of them understood that Chien had, in his past, been Viet Cong.

Chien realized that their camp was still a dangerous place for them all - and even he didn't know if they would run into trouble - be it from the local authorities, military forces, criminals, smugglers or others who were up to no good. In the back of Chien's mind, there was always the concern that there may be minefields.

As they explored further and wider across the island, he insisted that they flag their way back to camp with marker lines made from thin rope; some of which they took from their stock on High Tides, others made from vines pulled out of the lower branches of the trees.

A short distance away to the north of their campsite, they found a large freshwater pond where to their delight, the fishing was very good. The pond also enabled them to stock up with a clean supply of fresh drinking water which they took out to High Tides, ready for their onward journey.

Several times each day they would go back to their camp to check that all was as it should be and to prepare a large meal, which they ate as dusk descended upon them, to restore their energy levels. That was when Chien would usually tell them about lots of different world philosophies and beliefs, alternative ways for each of them to live their lives productively, profitably and well and at the same time how to stay strong and healthy and to help others.

Chien always placed great importance on the concept - the necessity - of helping those around you, particularly those who could not help themselves, either easily or at all.

After about three weeks of hunting, trapping, weapons training, shooting practice, fishing and teaching of all kinds, both mental and physical, Chien informed Hung that they would be leaving the island at first light the following morning and that they were to pack up most of the camp that evening, ready for early departure. Darkness was coming fast so they lit the campfire and all the torches.

They made a start on getting ready for departure, before bedding down for the night. The eerie and scary sounds of the night that came out of the nearby jungle had initially disturbed Hung a lot, but he was growing accustomed to them now. There was usually a good deal of moonlight, but that last night was overcast and the darkness was deep.

"Hung!" Nhât whispered.

"What?" Hung replied from under the giant banana tree leaf that he was using as a blanket.

"I bet you half my breakfast that you're a chicken shit coward," Nhât hissed.

"What are you talking about, idiot," Hung fumed. He

couldn't believe what he was hearing.

"We all know you're a wussy man and I can prove it!" Nhât whispered a bit louder.

"What are you talking about?" Hung asked again, getting increasingly irritated.

"I've left a flag out on the beach just beyond the far end of the trench. I bet you wouldn't dare go get it in the dark - 'coz you're chicken shit!"

"Fuck you!" said Hung.

"Told you!" Nhât egged him on. Hung let out a low growl, then lifted the banana tree leaf aside and stood up.

"You suck," Hung told Nhât, before stomping off, heading along the trench and into the darkness.

Hung could feel his heart pounding louder and louder the further away he moved along the trench. It was very dark and the noises of the animals in the jungle seemed so much scary now that he was alone.

He knew that Chien had told them not to go out of the trench without someone coming along for company - and particularly so in the dark. However, Nhât had wound him up. His pride had got the better of him: he would show that asshole that he was no coward. He crept forward in the way that Chien had taught them. He knew that it couldn't be far to go, but it seemed like it was taking him forever.

He skirted around the spike pit which had been dug out in the bottom of the trench, roughly halfway along. He remembered them setting it up to help keep the campsite safe from marauding or dangerous animals, so he knew he must be getting close to where Nhât had left the flag.

A douc screeched somewhere close by in the dark jungle, causing him to jump and making him think that his heart would leap out of his chest. Taking a couple of deep breaths to calm himself, he set off again, before clambering up the side of the trench. He certainly had found the right place: the flag smacked him firmly in the face.

Hung smiled a little, rubbing his face where the whip of the flag had stung it, then grabbed the flag, pulling it from the ground. "This will show him I'm not chicken shit!" he said out loud, mainly to give himself more courage..

Just then, he heard a low rumble like a deep, powerful engine coming to life, immediately followed by what sounded like someone, or something, breathing out - slowly. A very long, deep breath. Then the engine noise came again. Hung's legs started shaking uncontrollably. He was frozen to the spot. All he could hear was the engine - or whatever it was - getting closer and closer to him.

He started to wet himself: piss leaked from his body as his Fight or Flight response kicked in. Now was not the time to fight: flight it would be. He threw himself back down into the trench and bolted back in the direction of the camp as fast as his shaking legs would carry him.

The animal's orange coat gleamed faintly in what little moonlight there was. In the darkness, the long black stripes on the coat concealed much of its orange color. The tiger was tracking its intended prey. It broke from its stealthy walk into a trot. Hung ran through the trench towards the campsite, yelling at the top of his voice, louder and louder, then higher and higher so that it started to sound squeaky.

"Help! HELP!!"

His voice cut through the darkness like a knife, his legs running faster and faster with each step. Hearing his voice crying out, the bloodlust in the tiger was inflamed further and it leapt into the trench straight at Hung. It came up just short, but it swiped at Hung's foot with its claws, catching him with a heavy blow to the ankle. The tiger was huge, particularly in comparison to the size of Hung.

Hung's leg flew out from beneath him. The speed that he had built up from running sent him crashing into the wall of the trench, slamming his shoulder and the right side of his face into the rough sand.

Hung looked in front of him along the trench: he could see the spike pit that marked roughly the half-way point between where the flag had been and the campsite. The tiger was slowly inching forward towards him, ready for the kill. Hung leapt to his feet and started running again.

The tiger was readying itself to leap for one last pounce onto Hung when a shot rang out. The bullet struck the tiger in the left side of its chest, stopping it in its tracks. It fell, snarling, a few feet short of Hung. Hung froze: he stood there, rooted to the spot as the tiger heaved itself up and stared at him, blood running from its chest into the sand at the bottom of the trench, making a bloody mess.

The tiger crouched, lowering its center of gravity, ready to finish the fight. It gave a low, rumbling and menacing growl and leapt straight at Hung again. Hung offered up the quickest and shortest prayer - "HELP!!" - then ducked down as low as he could so that the leaping tiger passed just over his head, landing in the spike pit just behind him. He watched as the razor-sharp points of the short spears in the spike pit drove up through the body of the tiger, holding it there.

The tiger struggled briefly, then twitched for a moment or two, and finally stopped moving. Dropping down to his knees, Hung gripped his ankle where the tiger's claws had left two giant gashes.

The others ran up moments later. The children helped him up as Chien aimed the rifle again and put a bullet in the tiger's head to make sure it was dead.

He turned to the children and, in a voice quivering with both fury and relief, he gave them a long and angry lecture about how ignorance, carelessness and stupidity like this was unacceptable. They all, particularly Hung and Nhât, hung their heads in shame. They felt that they had let Chien down - Big Time.

He then made them skin and butcher the tiger all by themselves. It took them well into the morning to do that.

Sailing at first light was delayed.

CHAPTER THIRTEEN

After Chien had patched up Hung's ankle and they had finished gutting the fish they had caught, they worked together to load everything back onto the junk. Most of the crates of guns, ammunition, grenades and explosives had been loaded on board gradually over the previous few days but there were still a number of loads to paddle out to High Tides and heave up on deck. A lot of trips back and forward between the trench on the beach and High Tides still had to be made. It was exhausting work and by the time they were done, all four kids were nearly asleep on their feet. The children were then told to hit their bunks for a short rest before they got underway. They remained anchored off the island as the children rested.

Chien stayed on deck, gazing down into the sea below High Tides, watching the fish breaking the surface, trying to catch insects that skimmed just above it, before they spooked themselves and dived back down under the boat. Then he remembered something he had left in his quarters. He went down below to his cabin and fetched the silver cylinder that had he had first seen when it had fallen from Hung's pocket.

Hung had told him about the pack that contained the rest of the cylinders. He hoped that it hadn't got lost on the island during all the dramas and excitement that had happened to

LITTLE DRAGON

Hung - and to the rest of them. He went over to one of the cabinets and pulled out what appeared to be a light colored brick with a dull and cloudy surface. He put it in a steel pan and carried the pan and its contents out onto the deck.

Hanging the pan over the fire pit which had been lit earlier ready for their next meal, Chien waited a few minutes. Then, slowly, the brick started melting into a thick liquid. Chien went back down below. He rapped on the children's cabin doors to wake them.

"On deck!" he shouted at each of the doors... Immediately he returned to the deck. Seeing Chien at the fire pit, the children all gathered there.

"Hung, do we still have the rest of the cylinders that go with this?" Chien asked, holding up the cylinder - which he knew was a detonator.

"Yes, sir. They are still in the backpack Nhât carried," he replied.

"Would you go get it for me?"

"Yes, sir," Hung said, turning to go back to his cabin to fetch the pack that Chien wanted.

Upon his return, Chien opened the pack and took from it the materials he needed. Hung watched as Chien started assembling a bomb which he thought was going to be similar to that which he, Tranh and Duong had made for their fishing expedition. With everything that had been going on, that seemed to Hung to have been a long time ago.

"I have done this before, sir. It blows them to pieces,

though," Hung said. You don't actually get that many fish this way - or at least not many that you can eat," Hung explained to Chien.

"Yes: I bet the one you made had a rather dramatic effect. I have a feeling that what you were taught to make was a fragmentation bomb, one which is designed to kill and mutilate anything in its path."

Instead of packing a bunch of rocks and other loose items around the detonator, Chien inserted several spacers - small gaps - to allow for air pockets to remain. He then wrapped the detonator in a cloth and rolled it around in the liquid in the pan, before pulling it out. The liquid dried quickly and formed a hard shell on the cloth.

Once it was completely dry, he attached a length of the coil fuse and then attached a short length of rope with a weight tied to one end. Satisfied that he had finished what he needed to do, he looked at the children and smiled.

"This is what is called a concussion bomb. This bomb doesn't cut things up into pieces: instead of mutilating anything and everything, this bomb is designed to send out a shockwave that knocks out everything within an area all around it. Especially if it's underwater. Now... Everyone into the canoe."

Chien picked up the bomb, along with a few nets with poles attached to them. He put the bomb carefully on the deck of the canoe and laid the nets alongside it.

Paddling some distance away from High Tides, they found that fish were quite plentiful. Large shoals of mackerel and snapper darted back and forth like black phantoms in the sea below them. They were like shadows in the water.

After waiting a few moments, Chien lifted up the bomb and lowered it over the side of the canoe. He held it briefly on the surface of the water, then let it sink gently into the depths.

"Gently, gently - we must move slowly and softly now," Chien said as they started to paddle away from the drop site.

A few moments later a shudder passed through the canoe, as if it was shivering. Followed almost immediately by giant bubbles which burst out over the surface of the water, exploding into the air. Along with the bubbles were little pieces of seaweed and small lumps of mud. Sen let out a startled yelp as the canoe rocked violently, but it did not capsize.

Once Chien was satisfied that the canoe had settled back in the water, he looked over at the children. They were all as white as sheets, gripping the sides of the canoe for dear life. Chien tried to keep a straight face but couldn't. His smile quickly turned to something bigger: he couldn't hold himself together any longer. He burst out laughing.

"NOT FUNNY!!" All four of them yelled at the same time.

Having recovered - a bit - they looked out over the side of the canoe. Dead and dying fish were floating on the surface of the water in their hundreds. Unlike the bomb that Hung had made with the twins, almost all the fish were in one piece. Hung quickly grabbed one of the nets and, dropping it into the water, soon had so many fish in it that he could not bring the net back on board by himself.

"Damn!" Chien said, looking at all the fish. "That worked

LITTLE DRAGON

much better than I thought it would."

Within a matter of ten minutes, the canoe was on its way back to High Tides, piled so high with fish that it was difficult to paddle. By nightfall, they had a full stock of fish, crab, and even a small shark - gutted and cleaned and stored away.

They all ate their fill - and then tried to shovel in even more, to the point that they almost vomited - except for Nhât who did eat too much and so did throw up... Twice. They then played a few mind games - brain teasers to test how alert they were - before they headed below to their bunks to get some much-needed rest.

Hung turned away from the table to go with the other boys to their cabin. As he did so, Chien put a hand on his shoulder and gave him a big smile.

"Little Dragon: on that island, you were braver than any boy I have ever come across. You are truly extraordinary - exceptional. Remember to follow your passion - the beliefs that you feel strongly about - no matter what it takes. You will always get there."

Chien then let him follow the other boys. Hung started, then stopped, turned again and looked back to Chien with a broad smile on his face. He bowed his head to the man who had made him what he was now.

The following morning, after they had completed their daily chores above and below deck, Chien took the wheel. They pulled up the anchor, then headed out of the cove towards the next port along the mainland coast in order to pick up more supplies. Repairs and maintenance works were required to the junk and to carry these out, more tools and materials would be needed.

The wind was brisk and it sent them on their way at a good pace: they would be in port soon. As they sailed along, Sen continued with her schooling of Hung - at Chien's request - despite Hung bellyaching about there being more useful things to learn besides reading and writing.

Upon arrival in port, Chien set the children to the job of unloading the cargo ready for sale. While they did that, he walked the short distance into the local town to take care of some business he wanted to keep private. He approached a group of three older children: taking some coins out of his bag, he attracted their attention by waving the coins at them. They came over to him. Chien then spent about fifteen minutes talking to the three of them. He dropped a coin into the hand of each of them and then headed back to High Tides.

After helping the children finish unloading the cargo, Chien asked Hung to escort Sen into town, to the main bakery along the main road, in order to pick up a few loaves of bread, ready for their next trip.

Chien told Nhât and Kim to stay on board, to keep an eye on High Tides and the rest of their gear and also to organize the cargo that they would be selling now - for cash. That did not apply to the guns and other weapons that they had taken from the island. The children were not allowed to have anything further to do with that equipment: Chien would take some of the boxes away with him from time to time, but other times men would come to the junk, talk quietly with Chien on the quayside and then depart with a box or two.

The children were told to give a warning if anyone

approached the boat - and Chien put together a simple form of alarm system, involving lengths of string attached to metal objects that could be made to rattle inside glass jars which the children were to ring so as to give warning when visitors were in sight and if Chien was below deck.

Hung and the others assumed that he was trading the weapons for... Whatever he needed.

Hung and Sen clambered down the ramp from High Tides and set off along the road towards town while Kim and Nhât turned their attention with some reluctance to the cargo: their disappointment at having to stay on board was reflected in the rather sour looks on their faces.

Hung and Sen made their way into town, following the directions given by Chien. On their way, Sen would stop here and there, having spotting one thing or another to admire or to touch. It seemed that they had been on the island for such a long time and so seeing and hearing all the people and looking at the goods for sale in the town felt new and exciting to Sen in particular, although Hung also felt much the same way.

They giggled and turned this way and that, taking in all that was going on around them. In reality, they were starting to act like the children they were. That was until Sen bumped into someone - an older boy - and was knocked to the ground.

"Hey there, little cutie," the boy said, standing over her. With a smirk on his face, he added: "You're gonna have to give me something for bumping into me." There was no offer from him to help her up.

"I didn't mean to bump into you: I'm sorry. I'll get out of your way," Sen said politely, starting to get to her feet.

When she was almost up, the boy clamped his hand across the top of her head and pushed her down roughly onto the ground again.

"Now about that payment," he said, chuckling.

"Knock it off!" Hung said, helping Sen to her feet.

"Oooh!. What have we got here? We have a bodyguard," the boy said, as two more boys of similar age to him stepped up behind their leader.

"That figures. Here we go again," Hung said to himself, stepping in front of Sen, between her and the three boys.

"You're kidding me, right?" the larger boy asked no one in particular, seeing such a small kid step up towards him.

Hung started to push Sen back behind him further, hoping that they would be able to slip out of the increasingly tense situation before anyone really got hurt. Hung felt he had had just about enough of getting his ass kicked.

"Oh no you don't!" the large boy said, grabbing hold of Hung's shirt with a quick thrust of one of his arms.

Hung could not believe how fast the boy was for such a large lad. Having caught Hung unawares, the leader of the gang stepped fast to one side so that he shifted his center of gravity, turned and, still with a firm hold of Hung's shirt, threw Hung so that he ended up on the ground, flat on his back, in the middle of a circle formed by the three boys.

However, before they could do anything further, Hung jumped back up onto his feet and threw a straight right punch into the closest boy's chin. The boy's head snapped back and across to one side from the impact; he had been completely unprepared for the surprise counter-attack. He fell to the ground, unconscious.

The second boy threw a wild right hook to Hung's head but because he was off-balance when he did so and the ground was loose underfoot, he stumbled slightly, giving Hung time to side-step, out of the way of the flying fist. The momentum of the hook meant that the boy was unable to keep his footing: he stumbled again, falling face-first into the dirt road. Only slowly did he try to struggle back to his feet.

Hung started to turn to face the original bully but as he did so, he was struck hard by a fist on the side of his head. His vision blurred momentarily, which caused him to feel disorientated: everything around him seemed to be spinning. Hung too fell to the ground, his head thumping.

On hands and knees, Hung squeezed his eyes tight shut to try to stop the flashing lights in his head and the ringing in his ears. He opened his eyes again just in time to see Sen punching the first attacker square in the mouth.

"Leave him alone!" she cried out, crouching down in her best attempt at a fighting stance. The boy spat on the ground, then laughed.

"Wow! That actually almost hurt!" He rubbed his lips with the tips of his fingers, licking the small trickle of blood that was starting to run from the corner of his mouth towards his chin. He then stepped forward towards Sen.

LITTLE DRAGON

As the boy approached her, Chien stepped out of the shadow cast by a nearby building so that the boy could see him shaking his head: the prearranged signal to the boys that enough was enough. Chien then melted back into the shadows and the boy backed away from Sen. Hung did not see Chien.

"I've wasted enough of my time with you two. Piss off! If I see you around here again, you won't be walking away!"

With that, the two boys who were on their feet picked up the third, who was still out of it, lying on the ground, and took off.

Sen helped Hung stand up. He felt his head where he had taken the punch. Giving themselves a few moments to recover, they then returned to their task ordered by Chien: fetching the bread. They bought the bread at a store next to where they had been attacked and then made their way back slowly to the docks.

Climbing back on board High Tides, they found Chien sitting at the table on deck. He had tea and bandages set out, all ready, in front of him.

"You saw?" Sen questioned. Unlike Hung, she had seen Chien watching the fight from the shadows. "You watched and did nothing?" she asked, with disbelief written all over her face.

"Indeed I did watch, child. I set up a plan with those boys. Paid them a little too well I am thinking now!" he replied, rubbing his chin.

Sen began to storm towards him, red in the face with fury

and with anger in her eyes, but Chien held up his hand.

"Now hear me out, girl, before you let loose all that rage inside you onto me," he ticked her off. She stopped just short of his outstretched hand.

He gestured to the stool on the opposite side of the table, indicating to her to take a seat. Then he signaled to the seat beside him.

"Come here, Hung. I have become used to fixing your wounds and patching you up now, boy," he said with a smirk on his face.

"Yes sir. I do seem to have a knack for attracting trouble," said Hung ruefully. "It's like a gift... a talent!"

Chien began to laugh a low deep laugh that sounded almost as if he was purring like a cat. "That you do, boy. That you do," he said, shaking his head while cleaning Hung's wounds, one by one, then giving him a different small bottle - another of his medicines. "This one's for the headache you must be feeling right now," he said.

Chien continued to smile and leaned back in his seat.

"Hung, you've spent a great deal of time with me and my family. I've told you many things and taught you much. I've also put you through a great many tests and tasks, which you carried out without question. I must say that any man would be lucky to have you as their son. I am proud of you. I know you are young yet and may have trouble understanding what I am about to say to you, but I'm going to put it to you anyway."

Chien took care in what he said, wanting to make sure that

Hung's attention remained focused on what Chien wanted him to know.

"Yes sir," Hung replied, trying to reassure Chien that he was listening.

"I have seen how, without a second thought, you did all that you could to protect your friends. When you are old enough to want to have a relationship with a girl or to take a wife, I would be honored if you would consider my daughter, Sen."
Sen looked down to her lap, not daring to look at either of them. Hung looked at Chien: a huge grin spread across his face. Chien smiled back in acknowledgement.

"Yes sir," Hung said out loud. That was easy!

"You two can get cleaned up while I go back into town and pick up the rest of what we need. Send up the other boys from their cabin to come along and help me. Not that they'll be unhappy about that!" Chien finished with a chuckle.

For the rest of the day, Hung and Sen continued with the daily tasks that had to be done on board, while Kim and Nhât were pleased to join Chien when he went into town to complete making his purchases, carrying the stock from High Tides that Chien was wanting to sell and bringing back to the quayside the things that Chien bought. They loaded their purchases onto the deck - the tools, materials and provisions that Chien wanted.

The afternoon passed quickly as they heaved the supplies on board before tying them down and strapping everything in place. Attention then turned to the preparation of the evening meal.

LITTLE DRAGON

As they were eating, the wind started to pick up, blowing away the foul smells of the harbor. Finishing their meal, the children began clearing the dishes. As they did so, the skies darkened, earlier than normal for the time of year - and very quickly. Chien looked up: the clouds above them were dark and heavy and getting lower and more threatening - menacing - by the minute. Chien scanned the skies with a sharp and experienced eye. He looked about him, across the shoreline, the harbor and towards the sea, taking in the tell-tale signs of what was about to happen.

"We need to strap everything down tightly. Nhât: help me secure the boom to stop it swinging. We don't need it swinging back and forth: it could kill someone. This storm is going to be a nasty one. I think we may be in for a typhoon. Get the thickest ropes we have: we need to strap High Tides firmly to the dock wall and get more tires between the dock side and us to cushion the boat, otherwise she could be smashed to pieces. We also need to reinforce the bow and stern moorings onto the quayside."

Chien managed the children with authority: he had taught them well and they leapt to obey his commands. It was fortunate for Chien, the children and also for High Tides that the depth of water at the quayside of ports along this stretch of coast was sufficient to allow Chien to lash High Tides tightly to the walls of the docks.

Just as they finished securing the rigging and also strapping down everything moveable or loose on the upper deck, a flash of lightning exploded close by, lighting up the now almost black and threatening skies. It felt menacing: something big - something violent and rough was going to happen any second. The boom of thunder seemed to rock the air as the soundwaves traveled across the water, warning everyone of the fast-approaching danger.

The wind grew in strength and ferocity with every second - and the sea joined in, adding to the chaos by causing the boats around them to rear up and buck violently, like unbroken horses.

The heavier and wider hull of High Tides and the greater depth of its structure that was under water gave this particular junk more stability than the others around it, rather than being tossed around roughly in all directions, which was the fate of other, less well prepared, ships.

However, the waves were increasing in size and violence and it was clear that it would only get worse. Looking around him, Chien saw the roof blow off one of the smaller houses in the market area of the town, quickly followed by that from another house: the wind's strength was increasing all the time.

Chien turned to the children who were closing up around him and ordered them to head below deck. As he did so, the rain started coming down like a heavy curtain, drenching them and everything on deck in a matter of seconds. Lightning streaking across the sky and down to the ground so fast: it seemed that the sky was always lit by brilliant white light. The claps of thunder followed the lightning immediately. It wasn't a storm; it was a typhoon and it was on top of them.

Without warning, one of the other junks that had been at anchor nearby broke loose and slammed hard into the side of High Tides which faced out into the harbor. She seemed to soak up the crash without much trouble - and with little more than minor damage - but the smaller junk's hull crumpled and buckled under the force of the impact, like a piece of paper that is screwed up into a ball in someone's hand.

The lowest timbers of the other junk's hull splintered and split, drifting off into the increasingly rough waters of the harbor, while its upper deck smashed into pieces against the deck rails of High Tides, sending huge needles of wood and other debris flying across the deck - as life-threatening and dangerous as if they were knives being thrown by some unseen warrior. Dangerous to both High Tides and also to anyone who might be so unwise as to come up on deck.

Chien rushed over to the children who had stood frozen to the spot as the other junk hit High Tides. He pushed them into the shelter of the bodywork of the deckhouse where it stood high above the surrounding deck.

As he did so, more missiles that had been made out of the hull of the wrecked junk by the typhoon winds slammed against the open hatch that led down to the cabins, then slid away from the doorway, over to the other side of the deck, nearest to the quayside. If it had happened a few seconds earlier, it would have hit the children as they were heading below.

"Go below at once. Stay down below deck," Chien yelled above the now screaming wind. The children immediately raced around the corner of the deckhouse and rushed through the hatch leading to the central corridor which led to all the cabins. Following immediately behind them, Chien fastened down the hatch cover as tightly as he could.

CHAPTER FOURTEEN

Mother Nature holds wild and violent forces in her power. Bargains cannot be made with her, nor is there any way to reduce the savage strength that she can let loose - anywhere, any time, against anyone or anything. There is no logic to her actions. She is... pure power.

As the children made their way down below deck and the hatch was locked down tightly, the remainder of the wrecked junk was lifted up by the waves and the wind, acting together, and thrown again onto High Tides, smashing with incredible force into the hull.

Even where the children were in the gangway, with the cabins between them and the outside of the hull, the noise was deafening. They all covered their ears for a few moments, but then they had to try to brace themselves: the impact of the other boat threw them all against the opposite wall of the gangway, closest to the quayside.

Chien quickly grabbed some rope and straps from his cabin and started tying everyone to the bulkheads - the structural timbers - of High Tides to try to keep them from getting thrown about so much. The violent tossing and bucking of High Tides, which had become extreme, could easily kill them. It was as if High Tides had come alive and was possessed by an evil spirit.

For the next few hours, they hunkered down in the central passageway as High Tides was tossed and rocked by the fury of the storm outside. Luckily for them, they had secured well everything that was stored below deck and so few items came loose, although those that did became missiles to be looked out for and avoided. They could hear the typhoon doing its best, it seemed, to throw everything and anything it could at High Tides and to try to destroy it - and them. However, their ship had been built with love, care, good timbers and with purpose. High Tides was strong: she held them safe.

Eventually, once the screaming and howling of the typhoon was not so deafening and when the bucking and slamming of High Tides had calmed a little, Chien untied them and, with difficulty, they headed up towards the hatch to assess the damage. In getting to the hatch, they had to climb over one of the main bracing beams which had supported the roof of the stairs leading up to the deck and which had collapsed onto part of the stairs. Fortunately not in the passageway where they had been sheltering.

Chien pushed against the hatch cover and, having managed to shove to one side the worst of the debris, broken timbers and other wreckage that had gathered on top of it, he helped them all outside, onto the deck. Part of the side of High Tide's deckhouse had been smashed in.

Stepping out onto a still storm-swept deck, they heard people yelling and crying. Chien looked around him, stepping carefully over the wreckage and debris that littered the deck. All the windows in the bridge superstructure of High Tides and also those set into the side of the hull were smashed in and the cabins were flooded.

Some of the barrels containing the supplies that they had just loaded on board had come loose and these had caused a great deal of damage. Most of the other boats in the harbor were smashed and had either sunk or were sinking - or had capsized and were bobbing alongside, upside down.

Chien then looked over to the beach outside the harbor: some of the ships that had been anchored outside the harbor entrance had been tossed ashore and into the merchants' huts, destroying both huts and ships completely.

People were pulling men, women and children out of collapsed buildings and from wrecked boats. Others were making a start on the grisly task of dragging the bodies of the dead from the harbor - in the main, these victims were those who had tried to stay on their own, smaller, craft - hoping to weather the storm on board. They had been taken by the typhoon as if they were its food and their boats had simply disappeared - smashed into tiny pieces and carried away by the wind.

As if the people didn't have enough to contend with: now the stacks of bodies of the drowned refugees would become even bigger as the dead from the typhoon were added.

"We need to gather up everything that can be saved and which we can use again, clear the deck of wreckage and wash it down and then we can make a start on the repairs. We must be quick, in case the typhoon comes back - or another storm follows along behind it. That can happen and if it does, it will probably just as severe as what we have just been through."

LITTLE DRAGON

Chien spoke matter-of-factly, to try to get the children to snap out of the shock that the devastation and destruction were, naturally, causing them. Hearing his voice and instructions, all four children seemed to shake themselves before they split up and set about the tasks in hand. As they worked, the skies started slowly to clear. The heat and humidity kicked back in again, signaling that for now at least, the typhoon was no longer hungry and had moved on.

Once the deck had been cleared, Chien collected together from below deck the tools, equipment and timber that they would need to carry out the most essential of the repairs. They set to, patching up High Tides to get her back into shape - just temporary repairs at this time.

However, to complete the job would take weeks and a good deal of money because of the sizeable damage that the typhoon and the loose junk had caused. Chien's trading activities and his dealings in the market would have to increase to fund the work required. That's where the weapons that they had taken from the island came into play; the money that he could get from the sale of the guns and other military equipment would be needed.

Two weeks passed and eventually, they came to the end of all the rebuilding work necessary to restore High Tides to something like her original condition. While the repairs were being carried out, visitors would appear on the quayside from time to time. They were cautious folk, who seemed to appear, as if from nowhere - almost as skillful as Chien in the way that they would turn up and be seen standing on the dock side, without anyone seeing them arrive. Always quietly and cautiously, not drawing attention to themselves.

Chien told the children that if they saw such characters, they were to let him know at once. If he was below deck at the time, they were to pull on the string cord that he had rigged up and which was attached to a knife, suspended in an old glass jar and which he kept in his cabin - a simple and basic form of doorbell. Whenever the kids summoned Chien in this way, he would come up on deck at once and climb down to the quayside to meet the visitor. No visitors were ever allowed on High Tides: all business was conducted on land.

The children would see Chien talking with the strangers. Haggling over a price, it seemed. Everyone was after a bargain. A deal would be done: sometimes quickly, but on other occasions after a lot of to-ing and fro-ing, accompanied by many gestures with the face and shoulders and much and arm-waving. When terms had been settled, Chien would come back on board and go either to his cabin or down further into the main cargo hold, collect what he had agreed to sell and bring it back up on deck. Whatever he was carrying would always be covered by a cloth or in a bag.

The children never saw what was being sold, nor did they know the names of or anything about any of the buyers, even though some of them were visitors who came back to see Chien a number of times to buy more and more stock from him. As ever, the children knew not to ask questions.

LITTLE DRAGON

Soon High Tides was fit to go to sea again. Chien and the children had done much of the clearing up and smaller repairs, but the heavy lifting and skilled work, such as cutting in and fixing replacement timbers and the repairs that needed more experienced hands, was all down to Chien. He had help from time to time from an elderly local man - a skilled carpenter - who Chien had known for a number of years, when they were fighting in the common cause.

All was shipshape again and the rescued supplies that had been saved from the typhoon - and new ones - were on board and secured.

They had settled into a routine: some of them would work on repairs to High Tides while others fished, both for food for themselves and also to sell in the town, since most of the merchants' huts had been smashed beyond repair in the typhoon or their food stocks had either been blown into the jungle or out to sea or had been ruined by being thrown around across the ground, through mud and dirty water, by the storm. They either fished from the shoreline, a short distance away from the harbor or, when it was calm and the wind had dropped, two of them might venture out of the harbor entrance, into the estuary, in the canoe.

Very few boats other than High Tides had survived the typhoon so there was a shortage of those in good enough condition to go to sea to catch fish. Selling and trading allowed Chien gradually to rebuild his finances and to restock the supplies on board and the store of goods that he kept for sale. Despite High Tides surviving the typhoon relatively intact, Chien had lost a lot of his trading items which had been torn off the deck and he needed to re-stock quickly.

Chien was eager to set sail: he wanted to get back home

to his harborside shop. He wanted to see if the destructive weather had hit that area and also to find out if his marketplace shop and the shop at the harbor were still in one piece. If either of his shops had been hit - or, worse still, both of them - it would take a huge amount of time, effort and money to restore and rebuild them - and if the damage was too great at either of them, the losses might break him.

"Let's get the last of the supplies up from the quayside and onto the boat. I want us to be on our way before the morning's out," Chien announced to the children. "'We're going to be heading back home to see what damage the storm has done there."

The kids were cheered up at the thought of going back home - at least for a while. They all agreed that they had had quite enough adventure for the time being. However, they could see that Chien was worried about what the typhoon may have done to the shops.

Once everything was on board, Hung and Nhât released the mooring ropes and used long poles to push High Tides away from the side of the quay. Chien steered them out of the harbor, back to the sea, setting course for the home that they missed. They all felt that they needed time for rest and recuperation; they needed to rebuild themselves, as they had High Tides. They needed time to heal old wounds.

This time, Mother Nature was kind to them: no storms or other alarms and a calm sea and a steady breeze pushed them along at a good rate of knots. The children stood side by side along the side railing, looking down at the hull of High Tides as she sliced through the waves, carrying them towards their much-longed-for home port. The warm breeze calmed their senses, putting them at ease and giving them a sense of peace.

It seemed like forever since they last felt such a calmness. They looked up at each other: they all had big smiles on their faces. For once, it felt that any possible danger was so far away that it could not touch them.

At last, they caught a glimpse on the horizon of their home port - just a speck far away, but one which grew steadily until they could start to see the bigger buildings. All together, they made their way below to their bunks where they started collecting up their few clothes and other possessions in readiness for going ashore - home - as soon as they docked.

Chien slowly and carefully brought High Tides up alongside the quay, before tying her up to the dockside mooring posts with new, heavier and stronger, ropes and made sure all were secured tightly. Opening the gate in the side railing, he slid out the short ramp onto the dockside to allow the kids to take their bedding and other possessions from High Tides and over to Chien's harbor shop.

For the better part of the rest of the day, they went back and forward between High Tides and the harbor shop, taking off the supplies and other equipment that wasn't to be left on board and stowing it in the shop as Chien directed. They offered a prayer of thanks to the heavens that the typhoon had skirted past this region; they found that damage to the shops and the surrounding area was minimal: that which Chien found was limited to normal wear and tear and was easily fixed.

With the evening approaching and with everyone back on High Tides, Chien cooked up a feast for everyone to enjoy on their first night back home. The night was calm and quiet:

LITTLE DRAGON

there was not a breath of wind, but fortunately it wasn't too hot. Chien laid out the table on the deck in a rather formal way - really smart, in fact - a cloth covered the old wooden table. Candles were lit, their gentle and warming light adding to the comforting atmosphere.

Gradually a soft glow spread gently over them as the moon started to appear over the horizon, rising above the harbor. The glow gradually turned white and became brighter as the moon rose higher in the sky. They ate and drank until their bellies were full, then played games, lifting their spirits even higher. They loved it all. They felt like a family, safe and comfortable in their own home.

"We must have a toast!" Chien said, raising his glass.

The kids hurried back to the table, abandoning their game.

"A toast requires wine, children - so we'll have just one piece of toast," Chien said with a chuckle, laughing at his attempt at a joke. He was, even now, more than a little drunk.

"That might be a bit more difficult than you think, sir." Hung said, laughing. "You've drunk all the wine!" He tipped the wine bottle upside down to prove his point. Two drops fell out.

"Well, that explains a lot," Chien said, grinning and swaying just a bit, as he pulled a coin from his pocket. "Best you go get some more then, Hung," Chien said, flipping the coin into Hung's hand with his thumb and swallowing in one gulp the remaining wine in his cup.

"Yes sir," Hung said with a smile. He trotted down the ramp and onto the quayside, before turning and heading off towards the marketplace.

He remembered how, on the island, nothing could be done easily or quickly and how much effort and work they had had to put into everything when they were there. He was glad to be back here where it was just a short run along the road to get whatever you needed, so long as you had a coin or two to toss around.

Hung arrived in the marketplace. It was as it usually was; it never really closed. He looked around: while there was some activity, it was quieter than in the past. As it was now evening and businesses had shut for the day, most able-bodied people had gone down to the harbor entrance or to the estuary or were out along the shoreline, pulling the bodies of drowned refugees out of the water and off the beaches, taking them inland ready for burial.

While the worst of the typhoon had missed the harbor area and had kept some distance away from this part of the coast, there were still a few unlucky folk - victims of the storm and mainly the crews of boats which had been out at sea when the typhoon struck - whose bodies were adding to the number that had to be pulled from the water.

The finding and clearing of bodies had been going on for weeks - months - and Chien and the children had been away from home for a long time, yet still it distressed Hung: the waste of lives. The five of them had been lucky not to have seen any bodies when they had docked earlier in the harbor.

Hung ducked into the nearest shop and, buying a bottle of the cheapest rice wine they had, headed back out again without delay; if you have the coin, you get what you want. The moon was now high in the night sky: a full moon, shining brightly and drowning out the flickering pinpricks of light from the smaller stars around it. Without a pause, Hung started his journey back along the dirt road towards the harbor …

On High Tides and despite being more than a little drunk, Chien was growing restless, wondering why Hung wasn't back yet, since he was usually so fast with his errands.

"I wonder what's taking Hung so long?" he thought out loud.
"His full belly must be slowing him down," Kim answered, giving a reason for Hung being so slow, even though he knew Chien wasn't looking for one.

"He's probably just enjoying the fact that it's an easy job and a safe route home for once," Sen added.

The longer Chien thought about it, the more he felt that something wasn't right. A sense of dread came over him. He was getting worried and that sobered him up quickly. Having the feeling of dread was enough for him: immediately he set off, walking down the ramp, over the quayside and onto the road leading to the market.

Hung was almost halfway back to the harbor. He had slowed down, enjoying the warmth and calm of the evening. He was looking up at the moon and the thick blanket of stars stretching across the night sky. He couldn't imagine anything better than to be a star burning so brightly all the time.

One was particularly strong: it was some distance from the moon so its brightness was all the more pronounced. The darkness also seemed to be fighting the stars all the time, but against the darkness, that star still shone out brightly. It had its own power, which was too great to be denied.

Hung thought to himself: *"I'll be like that star some day. No one will snuff me out. I won't be choked or blown out like a candle."*

Just as that thought ended, he felt his shirt tighten around his body as he was pulled backwards off his feet. His back slammed against the ground as the bottle of wine slipped out of his grasp and rolled to the side of the road, unbroken. Hung looked up: a short, fat, heavily sweating man in robes stood over him, smiling with the sort of evil smile that shouldn't be allowed on a face. The man was puffing and panting hard.

"I couldn't believe it when my messenger at the shop came and told me you were there. I've run the whole way here just to get a piece of you."

Hung recognized the man: the Pigman. The man was sweating and red in the face. If anything, he was even fatter than when Hung had seen him last. He couldn't believe that the Pigman had run from his house to where they were now without passing out. The Pigman reached down and grabbed Hung by the shirt again, lifting him up off the ground: while he was fat and usually did very little, other than stuff his face with food, he was still a strong man.

"You've no idea what you cost me by taking what you stole. The gang that wanted it back and they tortured me for days!" he yelled, clenching his fist tightly and punching Hung in the face.

Hung looked straight at the Pigman, then spat a mouthful of blood directly into the Pigman's eyes, blinding him for a moment and causing him to drop Hung onto the ground so that he could clear his vision.

LITTLE DRAGON

Lying on his back again, Hung lashed out with his foot, straight into the Pigman's groin as hard as he could. The fat man squealed, clutching his groin, then he curled over and sank to his knees. Somehow or other, this did not disable the Pigman for long.

"Little shit!" the Pigman yelled, puffing and panting as he recovered. He was trying to scramble to his feet to get to Hung again. "I'm gonna take out every second of what the gang did to me on your scrawny hide, boy!"

Hung got up much quicker than the fat man and swung his leg again, this time catching the Pigman full in the face.

The Pigman grabbed at his mouth as the pain shot through his teeth and jaw. Some of his teeth had been loosened.

He saw through his pain that Hung was trying to run past him, to escape the revenge that the Pigman was determined to take on Hung. Rolling to his side, he reached out his arm and grabbed hold of Hung's ankle. He stopped Hung in his tracks. Hung tried to pull his leg out of the grip of the Pigman but he found that the man had a firm hold.

The Pigman started to drag Hung towards him at the same time as he struggled up onto his knees, then back onto his feet. Turning Hung around to face him, the Pigman swiped his open palm hard across Hung's face. Hung could feel his face starting to swell as the pain of a thousand bee stings shot across from the side of his head and into his mouth.

"You're going to pay for the pain and dishonor they put me through," the Pigman told Hung, pulling him close enough to his battered lips for the spit and blood from his mouth to land on Hung's face when he spoke.

The Pigman then threw Hung backwards as hard as he could. Hung's shoulder slammed into the hard dirt road, causing his head to smash down onto the ground with the same force and impact as if he had landed against a stone wall. The skin on the side of his forehead split open and blood started to pour from the wound, quickly forming a pool on the road.

The Pigman stepped forward, preparing himself to give Hung one last almighty kick to the head while he was still down, when he felt a sharp pain on the back of his head, together with the sound of breaking glass. Glass and liquid flew all over his head and face as the wine bottle shattered.

The Pigman wobbled and staggered as he tried to turn to see who had hit him. When he made it around, he saw Chien staring into his eyes with a hatred the Pigman had never seen before.

"Chew on this," Chien said, then jabbed his elbow, as hard as he could, into the fat man's throat.

The Pigman froze on the spot. He tried to spit, then tried to speak, but no words came out. All he did was gag three or four times, before sinking slowly to his knees and falling face first into the dirt. He didn't move.

Chien rushed over to Hung and, scooping him up into his arms, hurried him back to High Tides. He could see that Hung was seriously hurt - worse than any of the previous Beat Downs he had suffered in the time that Chien had known him.

The children, carefully and slowly under Chien's direction, started to clean Hung's wounds and tried to stem the bleeding from his head wound while Chien cast off High Tides from the quayside, out of the harbor entrance and pointed the bow down the coast to a hospital that he knew about, a short distance away. There was no proper hospital in their home town.

Hung remained unmoving. He was unconscious for the whole trip.

Luckily, the hospital was very close on the shoreline so, having arrived in the port nearest to it, it didn't take Chien long to carry Hung from the junk up to the coastal road which came down to the harbor and then to stop a passing truck to take them, as fast as possible, to the hospital.

The other three came too: they were sick with worry about Hung and Chien knew that they would only get worse if they didn't stay as near to Hung as they could. And anyway, Chien was not going to leave Kim, Sen and Nhât by themselves on High Tides in a strange port.

Hung was still unconscious when he arrived at the hospital, but his breathing was regular. The hospital staff admitted him straight away, only asking the minimum number of questions before they rushed Hung into a treatment room. Chien and the other children were escorted to a nearby room to wait. They were ready to be asked more questions: there were sure to be some, they felt certain. The staff would want to know how it was that a young boy of Hung's age was in the beaten-up condition that he was in now.

CHAPTER FIFTEEN

After killing time in the waiting room for hours, Chien saw the doctor who was treating Hung coming out of his room and walking towards them. Chien rose from his seat and met the doctor in the doorway.

"Is he OK?" Chien asked, dreading the answer that he would get.

The doctor was a thoughtful man: he could see how worried Chien was for Hung and so wanted to explain things to him clearly and calmly. He therefore spoke in an unhurried voice, slowly, steadily and clearly, to allow Chien to take in what he was saying - and also so as not to alarm him or the three children.

"Hung is going to be fine. He suffered a bad concussion and has some swelling on his brain that should subside in a few days. The swelling can be very serious in some cases but he is being kept under close watch constantly to pick up any abnormalities - anything that is wrong or unexpected - that may arise while we wait for the swelling is going down."

The doctor summed up: "He will have to spend a few days here. He is resting now but is stable and healthy as things stand. I suggest you all go and get some rest as well."

LITTLE DRAGON

Chien gathered up the rest of the kids and headed back to the junk, knowing there was nothing else for him to do now that would help. However, he couldn't let go of the thought of Hung in the hospital by himself, alone with strangers and no family around him. He wished there was more that he could do so he didn't feel so helpless. To steer his mind away from his negative thoughts, he tried to focus on the rest of the children, to make sure that they weren't thinking the same as him.

Chien didn't feel that they could stay in the port near the hospital: a lot of fishermen kept their boats there and High Tides, being bigger than the usual fishing boats, was taking up the berths used by three of them. Therefore, they had no choice but to sail back to their home port, which was the next one along the coast. As they did so, Chien gave each of Kim, Sen and Nhât an easy but also time-consuming task, all involving a minor repair or improvement to High Tides, so that they weren't sitting around idly, stewing - worrying about Hung.

Leaving them with nothing to do would allow negative thoughts to multiply in their minds. Negativity breeds negativity: their mindsets must be positive so as to create positive energy.

The children were wise enough to know what Chien was doing with them. They saw the sense in keeping busy. If they just sat around, getting more and more upset about Hung, that wouldn't make Hung better. They all put their full effort into their allotted tasks and worked late, until after the moon came up. Then, after having a bite to eat, they all bunked down for the night, eager for the next morning to come so they could go back and check on Hung. None of them really got much sleep: they all just stared at the ceiling, waiting for the sun to rise, signaling that they could go back to see Hung.

As the first glimmer of daylight filtered into his cabin, Chien rolled out of his hammock, packed a few things into his satchel and headed up on deck. As he passed by the doors of the kid's cabins, he knocked on them to signal everyone it was time to go and see Hung. He was a little surprised that he heard nothing from either the boys' cabin or Sen's: silence. He thought about knocking again, but changed his mind: the kids had been working so hard yesterday and they probably had been slow getting off to sleep, worrying about Hung. They might as well have a few more minutes in bed: Chien could get High Tides on its way without them.

Therefore, getting no response from either cabin, he continued climbing out into the fresh air on deck. There he found Kim, Sen and Nhât, dressed and standing in a line, waiting for their orders. They were ready to go. That's when Chien really knew he had created a true family with these kids; each one loving and respecting the others and willing to give their all for the family that had evolved in such a short period of time.

"Let's go then," Chien said with a smile, letting the mooring lines slip from the quayside posts and sailing High Tides the short distance along the coast again, to the harbor nearest to the hospital.

Arriving at the hospital, they made their way to the nurses' desk and started to inquire about Hung's condition. The lead nurse on duty instructed them to wait in the waiting room while she fetched the doctor. Within minutes the doctor came to see them.

"How is he?" Chien immediately asked, eager for news.

LITTLE DRAGON

"Hung's quite a boy," the doctor said, grinning.

Chien gave him a puzzled look. Then he understood: he realized immediately that the doctor could see in Hung what he, Chien, and everyone else saw. What everyone who came into contact with Hung soon came to see.

"He's definitely beyond ordinary. I reckon he must be unique - one of a kind," the doctor continued.

"Indeed, he is," Chien replied, happy and proud at the same time.

"Interesting tattoos. They tell quite a story. The tattoo on his fingers told us how old he is."

"Yes, he's had quite an eventful life already," Chien agreed.

Chien noticed the doctor studying the similar style of tattoos that covered the full length of Chien's arm and saw that he was drawing his own conclusions about the connection between Chien and Hung.

"You too have had a busy life, I see," the doctor said, noticing that Chien had seen him looking at his arms.

"Yes, we're kindred spirits," Chien agreed. "Flesh and blood. Even though he is young, Hung and I have been through a lot already."

"Hung is a strong boy and his body seems to heal so fast - like nothing I've ever seen before - which is great. He woke last night and ate almost everything in the building. We even had to have more food brought in."

LITTLE DRAGON

The three children were sitting nearby and listening in to the conversation between Chien and the doctor with open mouths. They began to laugh and chattered amongst themselves, taking the opportunity to poke a bit of fun at Hung's expense, particularly since Hung wasn't there to deny what they were saying, or more likely, pretend to threaten that he would beat them up if they didn't shut up.

"Sounds about right," Chien said, smiling.

"We'll need to keep him in another day or so, but I'm sure that we'll be discharging him in about 48 hours' - early in the morning, the day after tomorrow. We'd like to keep an eye on him for another two nights. You can go and see him now," the doctor concluded.

"Great! Thank you, doctor," Chien exclaimed. He gathered up the three children and led them along the corridor towards the ward where the doctor said that Hung was in bed.

When Hung saw the four of them walk through the ward doorway, his face lit up like a tree at Christmas time. The kids rushed to his bedside and all started talking at once. They all asked to touch the huge swelling, the size of a golf ball, that stuck out from the side of his head. Hung agreed, so long as they were gentle: the bump was very painful.

Chien stood back; he watched and listened, enjoying seeing the four of them laugh and joke together again. They were so happy to be with each other.

After spending about two hours of non-stop chattering and laughing and after the four children had, between them, eaten almost all of the rest of the food that the hospital had brought in to feed Hung, Chien announced that it was time to go back on board and to let Hung rest again. They made their way back to High Tides.

When they got there, Chien decided to risk the anger of the local boat owners: they would stay docked there, instead of sailing back to the berth in their home port, since they were all tired from lack of sleep over the past couple of days. There was some huffing and puffing from the local officials and one or two of the local ships' captains weren't happy, but when Chien explained why they were there - and when the gruff fishermen saw the ages of the three children on board - their annoyance melted away and there was no further opposition from those who had to find other moorings. No one took notice of the rules and regulations that the harbor officials were trying to impose.

The following morning, just as dawn was breaking, everyone knuckled down to work in order to complete their daily chores quickly. As ever, the kids rushed through their tasks, wanting to be going to see Hung as early as they could. As they finished so quickly and because it was too early to be going anywhere, Chien again directed the children into a few more, less time-consuming, repairs to High Tides. As they finished those, he made the announcement that they should all sit back, relax and take it easy. A day off was the order for the day.

The kids weren't happy to begin with, but calmed down when Chien said that Hung needed rest and, above all, QUIET. He would not get that with the three tearaways making a racket all the time. Kim, Nhât and Sen couldn't argue with that!

Chien went down below to his cabin, where he counted up the money that he had with him. He then put together a list of their supplies and trading stock on board which he would be able to sell for cash. He knew that the hospital would not release Hung without first having payment for his treatment. He knew also that the hospital charges would be more than he could pay.

While the children rested, he put together a small bag containing various items that he collected from around the various nooks and hiding places on High Tides. He made his way across the quayside, along the road, past the hospital and into the nearest town to see if he could sell off any or all of the contents of his bag. Maybe the hospital authorities would find it within themselves to release Hung in return for whatever sum of money Chien would have to offer them - or at least for a part payment.

Although he wasn't feeling sorry for himself, Chien thought to himself with just a little bitterness that he had had such bad luck for so long, it would be good this time to have fate on his side for once. All Chien could do was try his best, so on he went, disappearing into the center of the town, where most of the people were gathered and where he reckoned, he would have the best chance of making sales.

After several hours of walking around the town and bargaining as hard as he could, Chien returned to High Tides with an empty bag and all the additional money that he could muster. He went into his cabin and climbed into his hammock, desperately wanting to rest for a few hours before they would have to make their way back to the hospital to collect Hung.

LITTLE DRAGON

The sun brought a warm and bright morning and the children were all up and about on deck as early as the day before. This time each of them gave Chien's cabin door a few raps as they made their way up on deck. As Chien was getting ready and before he came up on deck himself, the kids were laying the table and were getting ready a small breakfast for them all, before they had to set off for the hospital to bring Hung home. The kids were so excited to be going to fetch Hung that they almost inhaled their food like little vacuum cleaners, without tasting it. Certainly, there was minimal chewing - if any.

"Pigs at the trough" was the thought passing through Chien's mind as he watched them, stuffing their food into their mouths as fast as they could. Of course, he didn't say what he was thinking.

As all the children were impatient to be going, Chien also made haste with his breakfast. Then they set off along the road to the hospital, Chien rehearsing in his mind what he was going to say to the hospital managers about their treatment charges and what he could - and couldn't - pay.

As they entered the hospital, they found that Hung was already at the front desk, talking to the nursing staff and clerks on duty. He was ready to leave - more than ready. Everyone ran to Hung's side and had a group hug. All four kids started chattering away, just as they had done on the previous visit. Kim, Sen and Nhât were all overjoyed to see Hung and couldn't wait to take him home. The doctor approached the scene with a smile on his face, seeing all the kids together and happy.

The doctor carried out one last examination of Hung and all his lumps, bumps, bruises and wounds, checked him over thoroughly and then discharged him. The hematoma on his head had reduced in size a lot over the past day and the bruising around his face from the punches he took seemed to be healing quickly. The doctor shone a bright light in each of Hung's eyes in turn to check the responses of his pupils. He seemed satisfied.

"It looks like he's healing well. He has my permission to go," he announced. He knelt down, directly in front of Hung. He stared straight into his eyes. "It's been my pleasure to meet you, Hung," the doctor told him, holding out his hand for Hung to shake.

"Thank you, sir. I am very grateful to you and to the nurses for taking care of me," Hung replied, smiling back at the doctor and shaking his hand with a firm grip, just as Chien had taught him.

Chien looked at the group around him and smiled, but he dreaded what would come next.

"Kids: take Hung down to the boat and be getting it ready for us to sail," he instructed them. "Hung: you are NOT to do anything but rest - or there'll be trouble!" With that, the four children rushed out of the entrance of the hospital - Hung a little slower than the rest - and set off back to the nearby harbor.

Once he saw they were out the door, Chien turned to the doctor.

"I don't have much money to pay you for what you've done for Hung, but what I have is yours, doctor," Chien told him. His tiredness, the worry he had had about Hung and what the hospital costs would be all made his voice tremble a little.

"Sir, you don't owe anything," the doctor replied. Chien was startled. He must have imagined what he thought the doctor had said. The doctor saw an expression of concern on Chien's face. Chien's eyes opened wide and he stared back at the doctor with confusion showing all over his face.

"You treated him for free? Why?"

"You misunderstand, sir," the doctor said with a grin. "A gentleman came in late last night and paid for Hung's care."

"Who?" Chien questioned.

"An older gentlemen who said he was Hung's uncle," the doctor replied.

"Where is he now?"

"He said he would be back early this morning but hasn't arrived yet," the doctor informed him.

"Could you tell him when - if - he arrives that we're berthed at the harbor down the road?" Chien asked.

"I will," the doctor said happily, with a nod of his head.

Chien thanked the doctor as best he could. The payment of the hospital fees by the man who was unknown to him had been a big shock for Chien and he was rather lost for words. He said what his confused brain allowed him to say and then walked out of the hospital and made his way slowly back to High Tides.

He stared at the ground, taking in and then trying to think through logically what he had just been told. The man who

LITTLE DRAGON

said he was Hung's uncle wouldn't have paid for the hospital care unless Hung's family wanted him back. The thought of losing Hung gave Chien a sick feeling in his stomach.

"What if he wants to go with his uncle?"

Chien did not like at all the thought of Hung leaving. All the teaching and time that he had put in with Hung, all the knowledge and skills that he had passed onto him, had resulted in the two of them forming a tight bond; one that he did not think that he was not ready to let go of yet. All the way back to the boat, the same thoughts raced through his mind, over and over again.

Chien arrived on the quayside where High Tides was moored and saw the children sitting at the table on deck, chatting and laughing. He still had no idea what to do. He climbed on board and, without speaking to the children, headed immediately down to the supply room, from where he collected a mix of fruit and vegetables on a plate; a snack for them all while they talked.

Making his way back up on deck, he still could not shake a growing feeling of unease in his stomach. He walked up to the table and set the plate down. The children thanked him and started talking between themselves again, this time with their mouths full.

Chien was turning away to leave when Hung spoke up: "Why aren't we headed back, sir?" he asked. "I thought you were wanting to sail back home straight away."

Chien turned back to face the children. He looked at the group with sad and worried eyes. The children looked back at him, confused. They were expecting him to be happy that

Hung was out of hospital. Something was wrong. They fell silent.

"I was told something by the doctor that I wasn't expecting," Chien explained as they looked at him, increasingly worried by the look on Chien's face. "When I went to pay him, he informed me that the hospital charges had already been paid by someone else. When I asked who had done that, the doctor said it was Hung's uncle."

Hung's expression suddenly became more serious. The rest of the children quickly followed suit. All of them looked at Hung.

"Where is he now?" Hung asked, looking at the top of the table. He knew that Chien was watching him closely, wondering why Hung had never mentioned his family.

"If you have family here or nearby and as you have been gone from them for a long time, they must be out of their minds with worry and will have been looking for you, Hung."

"I'd done so many bad and wrong things, sir. I thought I was just a burden to them. I felt that I was like a weight around their necks. I didn't know what else to do at the time," Hung told him. "Then I met you guys and loved being with you so much, I didn't want to leave."

Chien's heart sang with joy upon hearing Hung say that. The words almost brought him to tears, but he knew that he had to be both mentally and emotionally strong now.

At that moment something, a trigger in his mind, caused Chien to look up and across to the quayside. He saw a man approaching the ramp leading onto the deck. He figured it

LITTLE DRAGON

must be the uncle.

"Is that your uncle?" Chien asked Hung, nodding his head in the direction of the approaching man.

Hung looked over towards the quayside, to where Chien was pointing. Yes: it was his uncle. Hung wasn't ready to say anything: he just nodded back to Chien.

"Children, go down below to your cabins, please," Chien instructed. With worried looks on their faces, Kim, Sen and Nhât headed through the hatchway and climbed down to the gangway leading to their cabins. They didn't want to go into their cabins but instead, hid just out of sight of those on deck, straining hard to listen in to what was being said.

"Remember Hung, no matter what happens here, I consider you to be part of this family and you'll always be a part of us." Hung couldn't speak: he just nodded his head again.

Chien welcomed the man aboard and ushered him to the table where Hung was seated. Chien offered him the chair next to Hung and then sat down himself, on the other side of the man.

"Hello, Hung," his uncle said to him in a quiet voice.

"Hello, sir," replied Hung. His uncle was startled; he had never known Hung to be so polite.

"Your mother has been frantic with worry and looking everywhere she could think of for you," he began. "She would like it very much if you returned home. She has news she would like to share with you. She is anxious that you hear it as soon as possible. I think you will be very pleased to hear it as well. I would tell you myself, but your mother insisted that you return home so she could be the one to give it to you," he informed Hung.

"May I have some time to say goodbye," Hung replied.

"Yes, of course. I can see you've become very attached to this family." Hung's uncle smiled. "Why don't you come home tomorrow? You made it here so I'm certain you can make it back by yourself."

"I can, sir," Hung assured him.

"Very well, Hung." Hung's uncle stood and shook Chien's hand, thanking him for his care of Hung.

"I'll see you tomorrow, Hung." With that, he walked down the ramp and headed back the way he came.

Once again, they slipped the mooring lines from the quayside and sailed back along the coast, heading for the harbor and their home town. It didn't take long - certainly not long enough for any of the five of them.

They started to say their good-byes as they sailed. Sailing with Hung for what they all knew would be the last time. They understood that this was something he had to do. No matter how much they might beg and plead with him to stay, they knew it would make no difference, so they didn't really try. Instead, that night they used their remaining time wisely and played games, told stories, laughed and loved being in each other's company.

They were all blessed by the feeling of security and closeness that only the closest of families experience.

LITTLE DRAGON

Arriving in port late in the evening, they had tied up at their usual berth in the dock and settled down for their last night together.

When morning came, Chien was on deck at the bow of High Tides, waiting for Hung who was saying his final and tearful good-byes to the other three. Upon seeing Hung climb up on deck, Chien approached him and embraced him like a father. Then he looked deeply into Hung's eyes.

"Follow your passions, Hung. No matter what it takes, or where you have to go: follow your passions. Focus your thoughts and your inner strength and you can make happen whatever you want. Remember what I taught you and use it to your advantage." He embraced Hung one last time then followed him down onto the quayside. The other three stood at High Tides' deck rails, looking down at Hung, tears running down their cheeks, each waving a hand slowly, unable to speak.

"Thank you for everything, sir," Hung called back to Chien, before turning away to start the walk down the road in the direction to his village. He fought with all his strength to keep the tears out of his eyes. His lip trembled. His heart felt heavy.

Hung had been with Chien for nine months. In that time, he had grown in confidence, stature and maturity. The way he walked and how he held himself made him appear older than he was. He walked like a grown man - an adult. He had learned new skills, skills which the great majority of people would never learn. He had learned much of the ways of the world. All thanks to Chien.

LITTLE DRAGON

As he approached his home, Hung came up to the well that was a short distance from the bottom of the hill below his village. It was where they got their clean water. It reminded him of the first time that he had had to drag himself along another dusty road to get water from the well for Chien. The memory saddened him. He noticed buckets and a staff - a stick for carrying the buckets across his shoulders - lying next to the well. He had a thought.

He stopped and filled the buckets with water from the well. He put the staff through the handles and heaved the heavy weight up onto his shoulders.

After all the trouble he had caused, he figured the least he could do was to bring his mother a day's supply of water that she would need either today or tomorrow.

He started his climb up the hill towards his village. A journey that he had made so many times before. He felt the weight of the water and buckets on his shoulders: even though he was still very weak from the beating up he had received from the Pigman, he felt that the load he was carrying seemed much lighter now. He remembered how his shoulders used to be bruised daily from the journey up the hill. Now his shoulders didn't feel so tired. Despite his injuries, Hung was much stronger than he had been when he had run away from home.

"You're fetching me water. That's good," a deep voice said. An older boy stepped out of the shadows.

LITTLE DRAGON

The boy was much bigger than Hung. He was probably in his late teens and clearly outweighed Hung; he was quite fat so might have been as much as two or three times heavier than Hung.

"That's kind of him," another boy said, stepping out from the shadows, but staying behind the first.

"Yes, we'll have to thank him proper, won't we?" said a third, completing the trio of thugs.

"You have to be fuckin' kidding me," Hung said out loud, meaning to say it only in his head. "

"Shit!" he thought to himself. *"This is going to mean yet another fight."* His head and face still ached from the attack by the Pigman. He just wanted to run, but the three bigger boys blocked the way he needed to go.

Hung's heart started racing: he could see what was coming. His bloodstream was boosted with adrenaline. He felt his muscles tense. He let out a long breath - and noticed to his surprise that something strange - something different - was happening: this time he felt his body relax.

He looked around him, noting that there were no obstructions nearby and that he was on an open area of road: there was nothing obvious for him to trip over or hit himself upon. His mind became focused and clear: he was afraid but the fear was deep down inside him where it didn't seem to take such a strong hold. The demon in his stomach was gone - or at least it was under strict control.

Hung tried to get past the thugs by moving to the right-hand side of the road, but they moved in the same direction, blocking his path. At the same time, they gave one of the buckets a hard shove, which caused most of its contents to spill out onto the road. As a result, the lighter bucket on one side caused the load to become unbalanced. The heavier bucket slid down the staff to the ground with a bump, where a lot of the water was tipped out from it.

Hung still had the staff over his shoulders: he couldn't get it off him very easily, particularly because the buckets were still attached to it.

Hung struggled to regain his balance - a hopeless task, thanks to the unequal loads of water - and then tried again to move around the thugs, this time by passing them on the left side. The same result. Hung took a deep breath and let it out slowly.

"Oh no! Are we are making the tiny buffalo mad?" said the first boy, teasing Hung and making the other two grin and chuckle.

The first boy looked over his shoulder at his two friends with a pleased look on his face. As he turned back again to face Hung, one of the buckets hit him full in the face. It splintered into a number of pieces as Hung, hanging onto the staff with his hands, swung it around him like a windmill with the buckets still attached. It was as if he was in the center of a spinning fairground ride.

The razor-sharp pieces of wood scraped chunks of skin off the boy's face. The other two stood and watched in amazement as the remaining pieces of the smashed bucket fell at their feet. Hung then shifted his weight and swung around in a circle as fast as he could in the opposite direction, causing the second bucket to fly off the end of the stick and into the air, straight towards the other two boys.

They turned to run but before they could get out of range, the bucket struck one of the boys on his left knee, causing his leg to buckle under him. The boy fell onto the road. The boy fell hard, landing on a stone which stuck up a little above the surface around it. That caused the boy's knee to twist even more sharply than it would have done if the stone hadn't been there. The knee ligaments snapped: the boy's leg was now totally useless to him. The boy twisted and rolled around on the ground backwards and forwards, holding his leg and screaming for someone to help him.

Hung had kept hold of the staff and he swung it back to the right, smacking the first boy in the face again with the remains of the second bucket. The point of impact was where skin had been gouged out already by the first bucket hitting him, so he suffered even more agony. He too fell to the ground, trying to protect himself from the next blow.

The third, unharmed, kid panicked. He had got out of the range of the spinning Hung and his windmill. He reached down and grabbed a big rock from the side of the road and, more in desperation than anything else, threw it at Hung. The rock was so big that the teenage boy was barely able to lift it, never mind throw it, but fear had given him extra strength. He was just able to heave it far enough so that it struck Hung in the middle of his back - hard.

The rock was so big that in addition to feeling the force of it landing on him, Hung heard the "Thud" as it struck him. The impact slammed his lungs into his rib cage, causing small hematomas which sent blood spurting out of his mouth along with the air that had been in his lungs.

LITTLE DRAGON

Hung gasped for air as the blood gurgled and started to climb up his throat, filling his mouth. He fell hard onto the road. Hung rolled over onto his shoulder as the largest boy grabbed the staff and struck Hung across the face several times. The thug wanted to stay and beat up Hung some more, but feeling the stinging agony of his face caused by the splintered wood from the first bucket, along with the clout he had had from the staff - and the further hit from the second bucket - the first boy called his two friends to follow him and they ran off.

Hung tried to move, but still couldn't catch his breath. He tried to move his legs but when he did, agonizing pain traveled up his spine, stabbing him all over his body. "I have to get home," was the last thought that crossed his mind before everything went black.

Hung felt his arms being lifted up and placed, folded, across his chest as if he were dead. Then he felt an arm pass under him and around his chest. His head was pushed up and forward as someone began to drag him.

"Where are they taking me?" His back hurt so bad that he wanted to scream but he couldn't summon up the energy.

"Who are you?" Hung whispered in a croaky, feeble voice that was made even less clear by the blood in his throat, but he didn't hear any reply; he had passed out again...

Hung had come a long way from being

"Bụi Đời"

- a Child of the Streets. But his journey had only just started ...

From his time with Chien, he remembered

"Kiếp Nghèo Ôm Hận"

- that Poor Fortune Breeds Hatred - and he started to live his life to accord with that belief

THE STORY WILL CONTINUE...

Master Wong

is the Founder of MWS - KT3 System

His early life was filled with hardships and much suffering. Times were often sad and difficult for him and also for his family and those around him. The bullying and violence that Master Wong suffered as a child got him into scrapes and personal battles which adversely affected the quality of his education, causing him to leave school at a young age. His life continued down a difficult road, with many struggles and numerous obstacles along the way.

With the success that he has had since those times, Master Wong realizes that he can push the boundaries further and not just help people by teaching them his skills in Martial Arts, but that he can also guide people to build up themselves by achieving better health.

Good health comes in all shapes and sizes and Master Wong has learned that with health, wealth can follow - once body and mind are united. Dreams can be achieved once you have good health: strength in body and mind. After all, if your body was a Ferrari, wouldn't you fill its tank with the best fuel that you can?

It is essential to make health a top priority in order to stay focused in life.

"There are many ways to help people, but I don't believe in giving a man a fish to feed himself for a day: I want to teach a man to fish so he can feed himself and others for a lifetime! I want to show people how they can heal themselves from the inside out, and to help them build the self-confidence they need so that they can focus on their goals and dreams or find their purpose in life."

Despite adversity, you can work to overcome the modern-day challenges we face. His mission is to raise awareness, to help you become the best version of yourself that can be achieved.

DAD   HUNG   MUM

OUR MANTRA IS SIMPLE...

TRAIN HARD

LIVE CLEAN

FIGHT SMART

Don't let anyone take your lunch money!

REMEMBER ...

Time, place & a method of attack

ARE YOU READY TO START YOUR TRAINING?

Visit: www.masterwong.tv

CPSIA information can be obtained
at www.ICGtesting.com
Printed in the USA
LVHW051210260223
740443LV00009B/840